To JEAN

DECEIVED

FRED WOOLDRIDGE

authorHOUSE®

AuthorHouse™
1663 Liberty Drive
Bloomington, IN 47403
www.authorhouse.com
Phone: 1-800-839-8640

First published by AuthorHouse 04/26/2011

ISBN: 978-1-4567-2560-0 (e)
ISBN: 978-1-4567-2562-4 (sc)

Library of Congress Control Number: 2011900903

Printed in the United States of America

Any people depicted in stock imagery provided by Thinkstock are models,
and such images are being used for illustrative purposes only.
Certain stock imagery © Thinkstock.

This book is printed on acid-free paper.

ABOUT THE AUTHOR

Major Fred Wooldridge, author of the book I'm Moving Back to Mars, was nicknamed "Mad Dog" by members of his police department because of his ruthless and unique ability to infiltrate the drug world on the streets of Miami Beach. After working four years as an undercover narcotics officer, Fred was promoted to the rank of Lieutenant where he ran the Strategic Investigation Unit that included the Vice, Intelligence and Narcotic Units.

Six years later, Fred returned to the uniformed patrol division. After, the terrorist attacks at the Munich Olympic Games, Fred was subsequently sent to a newly formed SWAT school. He was promoted to Captain and went on to become his department's first SWAT Commander where he remained for the next six years.

When Fred was promoted to the rank of Major, he commanded his department's Criminal Investigation Division that included homicide, crimes against persons and property units. He remained in command of CIU until his retirement.

After retirement, Fred and his wife, Maddy, moved

to Highlands in the mountains of North Carolina where they started a seasonal rappelling school and taught cliff rappelling, entertaining visitors and tourists who came to this resort village looking for excitement.

Thirteen years later, they sold their rappelling school and Fred became a columnist for the Highlands Newspaper in North Carolina.

CHAPTER ONE

"Hey, Tony, you should pay me to eat this crap. People think cops eat in restaurants that serve tasty food. Your patrons feel safer when I'm around. I come in this joint to help your business and this is what I get?"

With no premonition that he would soon be drowning in his own blood, Captain Greg Strong stabbed his last bite of veal parmesan. He pushed the breaded morsel to the edge of his oval plate, scooping up the last of the marinara sauce with enthusiasm. Tony Vidalia smiled, turned his back to the offensive remark and continued to wipe the counter.

"It would make a difference if you ever wore a uniform. Except for that fake looking gun on your hip, no one would ever know you're a lousy cop. And for that smartass remark, Mr. Predator, I'm giving you a bill for the meal."

The other customers in the diner laughed at the verbal play between the two men.

Outside the diner and directly across Miami Beach's busy Washington Avenue, a rusty 1957 Mercedes, driven by a milky faced man with black hair pulled into a pony tail, rolled to a stop at a loading zone and sat with the engine running. The only person to notice was Mitch Hammond, a car buff, who had parked his UPS truck just a few feet from the diner's entrance. After a quick study of the car, he determined it was too far gone for restoration and continued to organize his roster of deliveries.

"Don't call me Predator," the captain growled at his friend. "I get enough of that downtown and I certainly don't need it from my friends."

"My, my, are we getting sensitive, big guy?" As promised, Tony slid a bill, face down, in front of the police captain. "And are we playing poker tonight, or what?"

The muscular policeman slid from his stool, picked up the bill and without looking at it, crumpled it and threw it at Tony, who caught it, a big grin on his face.

"Of course, my house, eight o'clock and don't be late. Maggie is making some kind of special snack soaked in bourbon."

Tony smiled, "I don't drink."

"Tony, it's a snack, for crap's sake. Don't eat it, just be there by eight. We're not waiting for you this time." Greg walked toward the door of the diner. The driver in the Mercedes pushed his car door open partially and placed one foot to the pavement.

Tony raced around the counter to meet his friend at the door. "Wait, don't leave yet, Captain. I almost forgot to ask. You know my brother-in-law. You met him last month at the church carnival."

"Yeah, I remember, Andrew, or something like that, right?" The captain took his hand off the diner's door and turned to face Tony. The occupant in the Mercedes slowly closed his car door.

Tony smiled, "That's right, Andrew. Good memory. Well, he's going to take up flying. I thought maybe Maggie could give him a few lessons, just to see if he likes it."

"Maggie isn't a certified instructor and can't give him lessons," Greg reminded him. "But each Tuesday, she takes a load of merchandise to Freeport. Simple stuff, like light bulbs. They cost a fortune over there and she has a couple of outlet stores paying her to make the runs. I guess he could sit in the right seat. Ask her about it tonight."

"Perfect. If this works out, you won't have to pay that bill you threw at me," Tony joked.

Captain Strong laughed and pulled the door to the diner wide open. "See you at eight."

The captain stood in front of the diner, fishing for a toothpick he knew was somewhere in his left pocket. Looking north up Washington Avenue he could see the time and temperature on top of the Financial Federal building. It flashed 94 degrees, 1:14 P.M., a typical humid August day for Miami Beach.

Mitch Hammond returned to the driver's seat of his UPS truck in time to notice the occupant of the Mercedes had again opened his driver's door, leaving it fully open into a lane of traffic on busy Washington Avenue.

"The idiot is wearing an overcoat. Now I've seen it all," Mitch muttered to himself as he fastened his seatbelt and cranked his engine. "Another Miami Beach wacko."

Mitch watched the man rush halfway across Washington Avenue and stop in the grassy median strip, his stare fixed on the burly police captain. Intrigued by his appearance, Mitch waited to see if he could add another chapter to his already long repertoire of events he had experienced as a delivery man.

The pony-tailed guy stood in the grassy strip separating north and south bound traffic and stared at Captain Strong standing in front of Tony's diner. Mitch looked at the man, then at Greg Strong, noticing the small gun on his hip. *What the hell is this? Is that guy a cop? There's something going on here*, Mitch thought to himself. Mitch Hammond couldn't believe his eyes. The grim-faced man, standing in the median, pulled a short barreled 12-gauge Remington pump shotgun from under his overcoat. The man lifted the shotgun to the typical aiming position and pointed it toward the captain. He fired one round, sending nine .32 caliber slugs toward his victim.

Two nine-millimeter slugs penetrated Greg Strong's chest, entering from his right side, collapsing one lung but missing his heart. Two more slugs entered his hand, tearing off his ring finger just below the knuckle and exited, with one slug entering the side wall of his lower stomach, shredding his lower intestine. The other entered the palm of his left hand, tearing it to pieces. Three slugs missed completely, shattering the diner's large plate glass window. Customers dove for the floor. Glass covered the sidewalk and floor of the diner.

Tony wasn't as lucky as his customers. Two slugs entered his head, penetrating through his left eye and the other just below his nose. Tony was dead instantly. Thick plasma, oozing from his head, pooled on the floor. Outside on the sidewalk the captain lay dying. His blood, mixed with the tiny slivers of broken plate glass, ran into a stream of slimy water from the restaurant's air conditioning drain. The mixed blood, glass and water ran across the sidewalk and into the gutter.

Mitch Hammond froze in panic at the wheel of his truck. Tightly gripping his steering wheel and unable to let go or duck for cover, he stared at the gunman.

Greg Strong knew he had taken a death hit. With his lung collapsed, he struggled to breathe and could hear the sucking noise made by his involuntary attempt to refill his lung with air. Instead, he was drawing blood into his lung and would soon drown.

Stay conscious; stay cool, he thought, as he pulled his small weapon from his hip. The hit man had moved from the median strip and was standing in front of Mitch's truck, just several feet from the fallen police officer.

In a move that surprised his would-be killer, the captain opened fire, emptying his weapon. Two of the five .38 caliber slugs missed their target; the remaining three struck the intended target, sending the attacker reeling back in pain, falling to the street in the northbound lane. Captain Strong frantically started to reload his pistol, pulling cartridges from his leather belt. As he shoved them into his weapon, one at a time, he realized he had lost a finger. Thoughts raced through his mind. *I'm fading. I've got to stay conscious, got to kill this guy. He's still breathing. He must be wearing a vest. How can he not be dead? Why is there never a cop around when you need one? Where the hell is Tony?*

Slowly the hit man pulled himself to his elbows and

stared at the wounded captain lying feet away. The man smiled at the officer.

I'm a dead man, the captain thought to himself as he watched the man rise to his feet and jack another three inch shotgun shell into the chamber of his weapon.

In an act of desperation, Captain Strong, knowing he was breathing his last air, closed the cylinder on his weapon with only three cartridges loaded. He would try for a head shot. When he closed the cylinder, he inadvertently caught torn flesh from his left hand in the weapon. His hand was stuck to the weapon and the gun was jammed. As if his sub-conscious had now given up, his vision began to blur.

Exhausted and unable to remove his chewed up flesh from his own weapon, the captain slowly lowered his head to the sidewalk to await his death. For the first time, he could hear sirens, but knew they would be too late for him.

The pony-tailed man stepped to the curb and smiled at his victim again, raised his shotgun with one hand and pointed it at the captain's head.

Whatever caused Mitch Hammond to be released from his frozen state would never be known. Mitch jammed his truck into gear, popped the clutch and shoved the accelerator to the floor. Even with the emergency brake on, the large UPS truck lunged forward striking the pony-tailed hit man, lifting him from his feet. The truck continued forward until striking a parked car, crushing the man to death. The killer's head rested against the windshield of the truck; blood ran from his mouth and nose. With a look of surprise on his face and eyes wide open, Captain Strong's would-be killer had met his match, killed by a gentle, twenty-four year old UPS employee. He had now killed a human being and would have to live with that for the rest of his life.

The first police unit to arrive to the call of "Shots Fired" was Officer Bob Malone, a one-year rookie who was just getting to the point in his career where he thought he had seen it all. He didn't know Captain Strong but knew of his nickname, "The Predator."

Malone was in near panic when he radioed, "Officer down, send rescue, code three and send backup...and my sergeant." Malone was so much of a rookie and so focused on the downed officer, he hadn't noticed Mitch Hammond still sitting in his truck, hands locked around his steering wheel, eyes straight ahead, and staring at the man he had just crushed to death. Nor did Malone notice the arrival of his sergeant who leaned over Malone's back as he examined the captain for signs of life. When the sergeant touched Malone's shoulder, the officer was startled and jumped up.

"Take it easy, Malone," his sergeant said. "Is the captain dead?"

"I don't know. I don't think he's breathing. Christ, look at his damn finger. It's missing."

In less than thirty seconds from Officer Malone's arrival, twelve marked police units and two fire rescue trucks arrived along with several detective units. While firefighter paramedics worked on Captain Strong, an officer called for the medical examiner and the forensic unit.

Mitch Hammond's hands had to be pried from the steering wheel of his truck. He was shaking uncontrollably. A homicide detective placed handcuffs on Mitch and placed him in the back seat of a detective unit.

Mitch asked, "Am I under arrest for killing that man?"

"I don't know, son," a detective responded. "Just get in my car until we can sort it all out. In the meantime, don't talk to anyone."

***

The private telephone sitting on top of Mayor Alex Harkin's desk rang once. He picked it up but didn't speak. The voice on the other end said, "The Predator is dead."

The mayor responded, "You must have the wrong number," and hung up.

CHAPTER TWO

Dried pieces of carrot, potato and celery, left over from Detective Bill Riley's lunch, had matted into his long, scruffy beard and moustache. Finishing reports that should have been completed hours ago, Riley leaned across his desk toward a nearby detective. "Are you going to finish those chips?"

"Keep your damn hands off my chips, Riley," the overweight, disheveled vice cop blurted as he pulled the bag closer and out of reach of Riley's hands.

"I should have had more than soup for lunch. Got to go out and eat again. Wanna come?" Riley asked the detective.

Waiting for an answer, Riley let out a loud belch which could be heard by everyone in the narcotics squad room.

"Ah, no thanks, Riley," the detective snapped back. "I don't like eating with you. You look disgusting and you always try to stick me with the damn check."

Riley laughed as he turned his back on the detective and mumbled under his breath, "Big fat slob."

"Hey, I heard that," the detective responded in anger.

"Where do you get off, you son-of-a-bitch? You've got no room to talk. Look at you, you're a disgrace to the force. Get a damn haircut, and shave off that filthy beard. What does your mother think of you, or do you even have one?" The detective paused, hoping for an answer before continuing.. "No, you don't have a mother, a fag spit on the sidewalk and the sun hatched you, you piece of shit. And try to change your clothes at least once a week and stop farting when you're near my desk, and take a bath at least once a month."

Detective Riley had left his desk and was walking toward the exit of the narcotics unit, right hand behind his back, displaying an insulting single middle finger. Once in the hallway, Riley was spotted by Lieutenant Carlton.

"Where ya going, Riley?" the lieutenant asked.

"Gotta eat something, my stomach is growling. I just turned in my reports to Sgt. Vines. Then I was going to drop by the hospital and see Captain Strong. They took him out of ICU this morning. Can I bring you something?" Riley asked.

"No, but come here a sec. I've something for you." Riley moaned as he turned to face his lieutenant to see him holding a small piece of note paper.

"Captain Strong has been through a lot the past fifteen days," the lieutenant scolded Riley. "The last thing he needs to do is wake up staring at your ugly face. Keep away from the hospital for now. Here, read this."

Riley stared at the small piece of paper: 914 Euclid Ave. - 2nd floor - pot plant in the window?

"You gotta be kidding me," Riley laughed.

"No, I'm not kidding. Go over there and check it out on

your way to lunch. If it's pot, grab the plant and put it in an evidence locker."

"Come on, can't I give this to patrol? This ain't the duty of an undercover cop," Riley begged.

"Take patrol with you. Besides, they'll wind up calling us anyway. Then you can eat. And Riley, once...just once," the lieutenant snapped, "I would like to be able to give you a directive and have you complete it without all the bitching. Just once...is that asking too much?"

Riley snapped to attention and saluted Lieutenant Carlton, mocking him. "Sir, thank you for this important assignment, I'll get right on it. Eating is the farthest thing on my mind...Sir!"

***

Uniformed Officer Tom Morgan pulled his marked police unit in behind Detective Riley's Mercury Cougar at 914 Euclid Avenue. Displaying the epitome of neatness, Morgan stepped from his car to meet with Riley. The two policemen walked toward the apartment building as Riley explained to Morgan the nature of the call, pointing to the pot plant in full view.

"You smell bad, Riley. What did you eat for lunch?" Officer Morgan asked.

"Just soup, vegetable soup, I'm starving, wanna go eat something after this?"

"Nah, ate already, besides you'll try to stick me with the bill and you smell too bad for me to eat with you anyway. Take a damn bath, Riley," Morgan complained.

Myron Shapiro pulled his front door open and was

FRED WOOLDRIDGE

surprised to see a uniformed police officer and a bum standing at his door. "What's the problem, Officer?"

Morgan spoke first, "You the super here?"

"Yeah, what's going on?"

"Who lives on the second floor right above you?" Riley asked.

"Excuse me, who is this person?" Shapiro asked, pointing to Riley.

"This is Detective Riley of the Vice and Narcotics Unit. Are you aware there's a marijuana plant sitting in the window right above you?" Officer Morgan asked.

Shapiro laughed out loud, putting both hands to his face in shock. "Marijuana plant? Are you nuts?"

"Not so loud, Sir," Morgan said, putting his finger to his lips to hush the landlord.

Riley leaned forward and tried to look over Shapiro's shoulder into his apartment. "What smells so good? Did we interrupt lunch or something?"

Shapiro announced proudly, "The best chicken soup in Florida. Want some?"

"We have time for one bowl," Riley responded.

Morgan grabbed Riley's arm as he moved toward Shapiro. "If you're going to eat soup, I'm leaving. Call me when lunch is over."

"Okay, I'll get soup later, after we grab the plant. May I come back?" Riley asked Shapiro.

Shapiro looked at Riley and decided he didn't want this man in his apartment without Officer Morgan being present. "I'll get a take-out container for you."

"So what about the guy upstairs? What's his name?" Riley asked.

"Name's Caputo, Tony Caputo. His first name is too hard to pronounce so everyone just calls him Tony. He turned eighty-six last Thursday. His daughter had a birthday party for him. All eight grandchildren were here. Oy, vey is mir, it was so noisy."

The two officers looked at each other in amazement.

Shapiro continued, "That ain't no marijuana plant, Officers. Caputo is from the old country, came here years ago. He hates dopers; loves this country. No way is that a pot plant."

"You get along well with Caputo?" Riley asked the landlord.

"Yeah, okay, he's a good tenant, pays his rent on time. Quiet man, lives alone, doesn't drink anything but one glass of red wine with dinner. Marijuana plant? No way."

Detective Riley walked back to his car to retrieve his binoculars for a second look at the marijuana plant displayed in a front window. Standing in the middle of Euclid Avenue, less than fifty feet from the plant, Riley raised the binoculars to his eyes and stared at the plant, hoping he was wrong. *Damn*, Riley thought, *that's pot. No doubt about it.* As he pulled the glasses from his face, he saw that a short, elderly woman, pushing a grocery cart full of food, was standing next to him and looking up at the window.

"You should be ashamed of yourself, looking in people's windows and in broad daylight. I'm calling the police," she threatened.

13

"I am the police, lady, now go away before I bust you for stealing that shopping cart you took from Food Fair."

The woman looked at Riley's police badge in astonishment. "There should be a law against people like you. How did you get on the force?"

Riley reached down and grabbed his penis through his pants and shook it. "Hey, lady, how can you talk when I have you by the throat?"

"You're disgusting. I'll report you," she muttered as she walked away.

Riley walked back into the apartment building, shoving his binoculars into his back pocket.

"It's pot, Mr. Shapiro, let's go."

The three men climbed the stairs of the old, but freshly painted building and the landlord escorted the officers to Caputo's apartment. Officer Morgan knocked on the door and, after a short wait, Tony Caputo opened his door. The two officers could see straight through the apartment to the pot plant sitting on a small stand in the front window. A strong smell of garlic filled the hallway and wafted into Riley's nostrils.

"What's this, the police? Is my little Angie okay, Myron?" Caputo asked with a heavy Italian accent.

"Angie is fine but these officers insist you have a marijuana plant in your front window," Shapiro explained.

Caputo turned to look at the plant and smiled. "Is not marijuana, is Italian pepper plant."

Officer Morgan smiled back at the short, stocky Italian immigrant standing barefoot in Bermuda shorts and wearing a T shirt too small to hide his bulging belly. "No, Mr. Caputo, it's marijuana and we wanna come in and just take it and there'll be no problem, no arrest, no reports, nothing. Just let us have the plant."

"It's not marijuana; it's an Italian pepper plant," Caputo insisted. "A gift from a young fellow who lives down the street."

"What is that you're cooking, Mr. Caputo? Smells delicious," Riley blurted out, no longer able to contain himself.

"Who is this hippy? He should be arrested for being a bum," Caputo grumbled.

"This is Detective Riley," Morgan explained. "He's a policeman from narcotics."

Tony Caputo looked at the officer in disbelief. Riley repeated himself. "Smells delicious. What is it?"

"My Stromboli....the best! My great grandmother, God bless her soul, gave this recipe to my grandmother and it's been passed down from the old country. Believe me, there's no pizza dough in my Stromboli. I'm the only one left who knows how to do this," Caputo explained. "My little Angie is not interested. She says it's fattening, but what does she know? She starves herself and my beautiful grandchildren. You would like a little taste, officers?"

Riley nodded with approval but Officer Morgan spoke first.

"No, Mr. Caputo, give us the plant and any others you have and we'll be on our way."

Tony's smile turned to a quick frown, "You cannot have my pepper plant."

"Look, Mr. Caputo, we can arrest you for possession of marijuana right now but that isn't necessary," Officer Morgan explained, beginning to lose his patience. He pushed Tony aside to enter the apartment.

Tony grabbed the officer's arm. "Don't come into my home and take my pepper plant; it's not marijuana."

"Take your hands off me, Mr. Caputo, or I'll place you under arrest."

Myron Shapiro moaned "Oy, Tony, give them the plant."

"No, the damn police cannot come into my home; this is America; this is not Russia; this is America. You cannot take a man's pepper plant."

"You're under arrest for possession of marijuana," Morgan shouted, pulling his handcuffs from his belt.

Caputo resisted and pushed the officer back toward the hallway, shouting, "This is America; you can't come into my home without a warrant."

The two officers struggled in their attempt to subdue Caputo, now resisting their restraints with all the strength he had in his eighty-six year old body. The three men lost their balance and tumbled to the floor. Caputo's head hit the corner of his glass foyer table, smashing it and cutting a small, deep gash in his forehead. Blood ran down Caputo's face as the three men wallowed on the floor. Officer Morgan's clean white shirt was now covered with Caputo's blood. Detective Riley was able to put his knee onto Caputo's neck and put handcuffs on him.

Caputo sat on the floor cursing the officers. "This is America; you can't come here and beat me up and steal my pepper plant."

Detective Riley stooped down so he could get right up in

Tony Caputo's face. "Shut up, you nasty little wop bastard, you're cutting into my lunch break, and just for that I'm going to eat one of your Stromboli. Maybe you'll learn not to call people bums. What do ya think of that, you nasty little shit?"

"I'll report you to the FBI, you filthy looking policeman."

Within minutes, Caputo's foyer was filled with several fire rescue workers and police supervisors, along with backup police officers from both the detective and the patrol divisions.

Tony Caputo, now sporting a large gauze pad taped to his forehead, was placed in the back seat of Officer Morgan's squad car. His marijuana plant sat boldly in the front seat as if it were proud of all the trouble it had caused. Detective Riley, passing Morgan's marked unit, leaned down for a look at his prisoner.

"Maybe you would like to give me that old recipe for Stromboli and I'll make sure all my Irish family passes it on after they wipe their asses with it."

Caputo looked at Riley with hatred. "Vaffanculo, you're going to hell."

Riley smiled, "I took a couple of extra Stromboli off your counter to tide me over while I write a mountain of reports, you dumb asshole. I also pissed on your couch just before I left. That outta smell real good by the time you get out of jail, you fat little wop son-of-a-bitch."

Officer Morgan shook his head, looking at Riley. "Why does every call I go on with you turn to shit, Riley?"

Riley turned toward Morgan and gestured, "What, this is all my fault?"

***

The next morning, Riley arrived at work to find someone had tied small red peppers all over the confiscated marijuana plant. It was sitting right in the middle of his desk with a note attached which read, *To Riley from Tony. Hope you enjoy my pepper plant. All is forgiven. Love, Tony.* Detectives in the narcotics unit pretended to be busy with paperwork as Riley scanned the room for the culprit.

"Okay, who's the smartass?" Riley shouted.

You could hear a pin drop in the room, except for a couple of detectives laughing under their breath.

After a moment, Detective Dana Anderson, sitting on the opposite side of the room, called out without looking up from her desk. "I think the guy's got a thing for you, Riley."

CHAPTER THREE

At 3:18 AM the opening of the elevator doors broke the silence in the hallway of Cedars of Lebanon Hospital's eighth floor. Out stepped Special Agent in Charge "Big Ben" Turner and a uniformed hospital security guard. Walking to the nurse's desk, Turner pulled his identification from his coat pocket. "I'm Special Agent in..."

"I knows who you are", the nurse interrupted. "They said you was comin'. Down that hallway, room 820," the nurse pointed without looking up from her magazine.

Not used to such disrespect, the special agent asked, "And may I ask what is your name?"

The heavy-set nurse looked up from her magazine, exposing her large jowls and a huge double chin. Pointing to her name plate, she spoke. "Johnson...common spelling."

The two glared at one another for several seconds and then the agent turned and walked down the corridor, his leather soles clicking against the highly buffed tile floor.

The guard leaned across the counter and whispered,

"What da ya think, Lucinda, is the shit about to hit the fan?"

"I don't much care; don't like the Feds anyway, especially narcotic cops. Whatever he gets, he deserves and a lot more. And you know what's funny? They're going to give that police captain down on the fifth floor a medal when he gets outta here. They're going to put the scumbag in 820 in jail...after they fire him. Strong...I think his name is Captain Strong. When I looked in on him a couple days ago he didn't look too strong to me," she laughed, continuing to look at her magazine.

Ben's huge frame filled the doorway to room 820. The darkened room was lit by several small monitoring devices that flashed from green to white. "No need to pretend to be asleep, Pete, I see your eyelids fluttering. Mind if I turn on a light?"

Pete Spoto opened a right eye to look up at his boss, now looming over him. "That one over there, the small one on the wall. Turn on that one. What time is it?"

"About three thirty," Turner responded. "Can I raise your bed or will it hurt too much?"

"Nah, I'll do it. Three thirty? Have you no respect for the sick?" Spoto kidded.

Turner walked to Spoto's bed and spoke. "The hospital called me at home and said you were conscious. I came right away, against the advice of the inspection team, I might add."

"Oh, Christ, Ben, the inspection team, don't say that. How bad is it?"

Turner chuckled, "How bad is it? You have a fractured

skull, a broken collar bone, six broken ribs and you've been unconscious for three days. That's how bad it is."

"No, no, not that," Pete spoke. "I know I'm all busted up, I mean the inspection team, how bad is it?"

Ben walked to the end of Pete's bed and leaned over to get a better look at Pete's broken body, head bandaged, shoulder in a cast and numerous small cuts on his rugged, weathered face. "How long have we known each other, Pete, twenty five years?"

"Crap, Ben, don't talk to me that way 'cause I know it's bad. Where's Dianne?"

"You're changing the subject, Pete, which is what you like to do when you're in trouble. Dianne sat here for three days, slept on that other bed, waiting for you to wake up. When you didn't, she went home about eight last night. She's worried sick about you. She doesn't even know you're conscious."

Ben walked to a small table in the corner of the room that displayed two bouquets of flowers, both from Pete's wife.

"Hell, if I'm in the jackpot, she should be here. Am I in the jackpot? The truth now," Spoto demanded.

"Okay, Pete, the truth. Let's see, you sat in the 1800 Lounge until seven in the morning. They closed and threw you out because you refused to leave. You got into a government issued car and drove through a red light at Biscayne and NE 4th Street, then broadsided another car with a lady and her daughter in it. Not just any lady and her daughter, but Evelyn Knight, as in Knight, Stansel, Arkin and Ritter. You know, the wife of Robert Knight, who runs the biggest personal injury law firm in Miami, the same Evelyn Knight who is President of the Women's Democratic Club, Chairman of the

Dade County March of Dimes, on the Governor's committee for stiffer penalties for drunk drivers…that Evelyn Knight!"

Pete put his one good hand to his forehead and closed his eyes before asking the next question.

"Did she get hurt, Ben, is everyone alive?"

Turner looked down and away from Pete. "She's one floor below you, recovering from surgery. They took out one of her kidneys and repaired a ruptured spleen. Her eight year old daughter lost her front teeth and a piece of her eyelid, but other than that, they're fine."

Pete responded, looking for any possible defense. "They should have been wearing seat belts; they couldn't have been wearing seat belts."

"No one wears seat belts. You weren't wearing yours," Ben said with anger.

As the two men stared at each other, a look of despair filled Pete's face as the realization of what had occurred filled his head.

"There's more, Pete," Turner continued. "Your blood alcohol level was .19. The doctors were astounded you could remain conscious and still operate a motor vehicle but, of course, they don't know you like we do. And it gets worse, there are two eye witnesses to your plowing into the Knight car who will testify you ran the light, then got out of your car and fell flat on your face in the street. Now, Pete, let me ask you. Are you in the jackpot, or what?"

Pete Spoto knew the ramifications of what his friend and boss was telling him. He asked in desperation, "Who ordered the inspection team? Are they gone? Why don't you call Washington and talk to Levinson for me. Tell him I'll quit drinking; desk duty for a year. I'll pay the hospital bills. I'll do another year in Colombia, whatever they want," Pete rambled on.

Ben reached out to touch the arm of his long-time friend, "I called Levinson. I had to, under the circumstances, and he ordered the Inspection Team to Miami, Pete. I already promised Levinson you would quit drinking last year after you tore up the Barbary Coast Bar. They're going to fire you, Pete, no deals, no more sending you overseas, no more desk duty. They're going to fire you and there's not a damn thing I or anyone else can do about that."

Turner turned loose of Spoto's arm and continued. "The heat is too severe. The press is having a field day with this because we look so bad. This is going to cost DEA a bundle of money. Everyone's pissed at you, Pete, including me. I love you like my own brother, but I can't save you, not this time. You're the best undercover agent DEA has ever had. No one will take that from you, but Washington now sees you as a loose cannon, a double edged sword, now cutting the wrong way. You know I'm the last person in the world to back Levinson; hell, he wouldn't know a drug dealer if one sat in his lap, but this time he's right. He has no choice. You've put us all in a bad position. Can you see that, Pete?"

There was silence as Pete drank in and digested all he had just heard. His head was splitting and his shoulder was throbbing. After a moment, Pete spoke, "I need a pain pill. Ben, let me ring for the nurse. Where's the damn button? How is Katy?" Pete asked as he combed the bed with his one good arm, searching for the emergency alert button. "She must've been pissed when the hospital woke you at that time of the morning. I know you must've told her about this. I know she's disappointed in me. Does Levinson know I'm the godfather of your kid?" Pete rambled on. "Does he care anything about that? Where in the hell is the button? How about when I tanked Esposito and got the Agent of the Year award? Does the agency know how much dope we took off the street on that one?"

Pete continued to grope around the bed with one hand, looking for the button to ring for help. "And how about when I took a bullet from that rookie agent whose mother was a state representative or something like that? I said nothing. I covered DEA's ass on that one and how about when they couldn't find anyone stupid enough to volunteer for that assignment in Texas that was doomed to failure? I almost lost my life on that one. Does any of that count, Ben, does any of that count?"

Ben backed away from the bed and put both hands into his pockets, staring at the hospital floor. "It's attached to the rail."

"What's attached to the rail, what does that mean?"

"The buzzer, it's attached to the bed rail."

Pete's eyes were wet with tears, fighting back a full cry with all the inner strength he had.

"I'm going down to talk to the Knight woman. Maybe when she sees what she's doing and realizes she's ending my whole career or my whole life, she'll change her mind," Pete said.

"It's not the woman's decision Pete; it's DEA's decision. I'm sorry for you. I'm angry at you and I feel so bad for you at the same time."

24

Pete's head was filled with thoughts and ideas which he blurted out as they came into his mind. Excited and scared, he raised his voice. "I don't need your damn pity, I need the nurse. Where's the damn nurse? I've pushed this damn thing over and over and no one's coming. Where the hell is she? I'll get Joel Hartshorne to defend me. He'll find a way to save me, you watch. You know how many times that guy whipped my ass in court? Now he can defend me. Please, Ben, go out there and get me a damn nurse."

"Hartshorne won't take this and you can't afford him anyway," Ben whispered, hoping it wouldn't stress Pete further.

"Call him for me, Ben, do that for me. Call him."

"When I get back to the office, Pete, I'll call him. We have a block on your room and phone to keep the press away, so I'll stop at the switchboard on the way out and approve Hartshorne to get through, but don't count on him calling. Get well, Pete. Try not to forget the fact that I'm with you on this until the end. You'll always be my friend, regardless of what happens on this. I would do anything to change this for you."

Tears streamed down Pete's cheeks. "You're the best friend anyone could ask for, Ben. Please figure out a way to get me out of this and call Dianne for me, will you? And don't tell her or anyone at the office that I lost it like this, promise me!"

Ben turned in the doorway to face his old friend. "I won't say a thing, Pete, I promise."

As Ben walked toward the elevator, he heard Pete call out, "And don't forget to find a damn nurse."

***

Even though it was a short ride from Cedars of Lebanon Hospital to the DEA building in downtown Miami, Ben had time to ponder his friend's plight. He thought of their lasting friendship and all the incredible work Pete had performed over his long career. DEA was about to dump the best agent in its history. The academy was filled with cases Pete had worked, using them as examples of how to properly conduct narcotics investigations.

Even though rookie agents may have never met Pete Spoto, they left the academy idolizing him and looked to model themselves after him. He was a worldwide role model for DEA. The ugly part of Pete's career was that he had been in trouble often, due to his out-of-control personality. The very things that made Pete a great DEA agent were the same things that got him in continuous trouble. For certain, there would never be another man like him again. *What a waste*, Ben thought as he turned the corner onto 12th Street and approached his office building.

Ben pulled a small device from his pocket and aimed it. The large heavy metal door to DEA's garage opened, making a terrible racket and startling several winos sleeping nearby. To Ben's surprise, there stood Assistant Special Agent in Charge, Tom Zernheld, Ben's second in command.

What is Tom doing in the garage at this time of the morning, Ben wondered as he pulled into his assigned parking slot and drove forward until his front bumper came within inches of Zernheld's pants. Ben opened his car door and leaned out to listen to what Tom might have to tell him.

Tom spoke with urgency in his voice that surprised Ben. "I missed you at the hospital, sir, but you had just left."

"Sir; you're calling me sir? What's up, Tom, you don't call me sir when we're alone in the garage at five in the morning," Ben chuckled. "You haven't been in the office at this hour for a long time. Must be important or did Cindy throw you out again?"

Ben gathered up his briefcase and pulled himself from the vehicle.

"Let's go to your office; I think you should be sitting down to hear this and I don't want to talk in the garage," Tom insisted.

The two men entered the garage elevator and stood silent as the doors closed. Then Ben spoke, "This has got to be bad from the terrible look on your face. Try to relax, Tom. What could be so bad?"

"You'll see, Ben, you'll see." The elevator doors opened on the top floor and the two men walked down the dimly lit corridor past the cleaning crew and into Ben's office.

Ben chose not to sit behind his desk in an effort to keep the meeting as informal and friendly as possible.

"Okay, let's have it, Tom," Ben asked.

"Ben, I got a call from Levinson at home. He tried to reach you and Katy told him you had gone to the hospital. Then he called me."

Silence prevailed again as the two men stared at each other.

"Soooo, what is it, Tom?" Ben asked again.

"Well, Ben, I'm just going to say it. Nixon wants to see Spoto."

27

"What do you mean, Nixon, what Nixon?" Ben asked.

Tom leaned forward in this chair, bracing his elbows on its arms. "Nixon, as in President of the United States, that Nixon, wants to visit with Pete Spoto."

Ben leaned forward in his chair and the two men were now staring into each other's eyes from just a foot apart. Then Ben broke into laughter, leaning back in his chair, clapping his hands. "President Richard Milhous Nixon wants to visit with Special Agent Peter S. Spoto. Is that why you're out of bed at this time of the morning, to tell me that?"

"It's worse than that, Ben. Levinson is in a full-blown panic. No one has the balls to tell Nixon that they just fired Spoto," Tom explained.

"Wait, you're going too fast. Why does Nixon want to talk to Spoto? I'm sure it's not about the accident," Ben laughed.

"Stop laughing, Ben, this is serious shit. Wait until I tell you the rest. Levinson has already started the paperwork to un-fire Spoto. He intends to put him on paid leave until he is well enough to go to Washington. Then, after the visit with Nixon, Levinson plans to fire him again."

Ben Turner was now laughing even harder, "Levinson is such an idiot. If they do that, Spoto, as much as he loves this agency, will take that information and go public with it, nailing DEA even worse than the publicity on the accident."

"I agree, Ben. That's why this is so damn scary. You've got to advise Levinson not to do this. Tell him to tell Nixon the truth and cool things down."

"No, Tom, Pete is my closest friend. The guy is my kid's godfather, for crap's sake. I'm in no mood to save Levinson's ass at the expense of sacking Spoto. You, Tom Zernheld, will keep your mouth shut on this, do you understand?"

"Yes, sir, and to be honest with you, this is too political for me. I need to get out of the loop."

"Good, you're out of the loop as of right now. I'll handle this. Forget you got a phone call from Levinson. Not a word to anyone in this office about this. Do you understand?"

"Yes, sir," Tom said with relief.

"Good, now tell me why Nixon wants to see Spoto," Ben asked.

"Well, it's not clear, but it seems the president got his hands on that Colombian report, the thing with the Macedo cartel, and was so impressed with Pete's undercover work and his past efforts with that drug deal in Cuba that he wants to meet him and give him some kind of special award. It's not clear yet, but they want to do a big thing with the press, leaving Pete's picture and name out, of course, but highlighting his many accomplishments."

Grim faced Tom Zernheld looked to the floor and shook his head. "Ben, the man just crippled a woman and child and was so drunk he couldn't walk. Now the President of the United States is going to give him an award and you sit there and laugh about the whole thing. I know he's your friend, but this is going to get real ugly. This will eventually turn bad for DEA."

"It already has, Tom, it already has. If Levinson decides to tell Nixon the truth, I'll personally sink Levinson by making public the fact that he was willing to un-fire a drunk who injured two people to save face with the president. Levinson would have to resign. On the other hand, if Spoto has his visit with Nixon, they'll never be able to fire him. So Levinson, the guy who's running this whole shebang, has already put DEA and himself between the old proverbial rock and a hard place. We are spectators. And let's not forget about the Knights. When Robert and Ellen Knight learn we're not going to fire Pete, but, instead, give him an award, the shit will hit the fan and lots of pressure will be placed on Levinson to change his mind, but he can't because he doesn't have the balls to tell Nixon the truth. To be honest, Levinson is in more trouble than Pete."

Ben stood and walked to the coffee pot on a table next to his desk. "You wanna know something, Tom? I've always said and you've heard me say this a hundred times, Pete Spoto has one hell of a powerful guardian angel that covers his ass on everything. How many times has this man been against the wall and escaped the fatal bullet? And now the damn president of the United States is unwittingly going to save his ass. I need coffee. I need to think this out."

CHAPTER FOUR

TWO MONTHS LATER

Mayor Harkin walked to the podium, looked at his notes and hesitated before speaking. "Ladies and gentlemen, it is with great pleasure that I stand before you this morning... Just over seven weeks ago, when our city was in the midst of the Democratic National Convention, one of our finest officers was gunned down in the street just a short distance from this stage."

The mayor turned from the podium and pointed north with his arm straight forward, indicating the direction of the shooting. He could work a crowd better than any politician. Mayor Harkin paused, continuing to hold his arm out, pointing north and saying nothing, allowing his audience to absorb what he had said. Then he continued.

"Captain Gregory Strong, Commander of our SWAT teams and Chief of our Narcotics and Dangerous Drugs Unit, became the target of a murderous assassin but miraculously escaped death. Thanks to the aid and assistance of our very fine fire rescue units he is alive and with us this morning."

The mayor paused again, looking out at the crowd as a shepherd looks over his sheep. "But this does not tell the full story. There's a man among us, an everyday citizen and a family man, dedicated to his work, who is our real hero today. Not only are we gathered here to wish Captain Strong a heart-warming farewell on his retirement, but also to honor a hero. As Mayor of the City of Miami Beach, it is an honor that I introduce you to UPS employee Mitchell Hammond. Please come up, Mitch. Captain Strong, would you come forward also?" The crowd broke into loud applause.

Greg Strong had fallen asleep in his wheelchair at the far corner of the stage. He was awakened by the motion of his wheelchair as Maggie pushed him forward toward the podium. He tried to straighten himself in his chair. His face was pale and gaunt. He had to force a smile as he looked out on the crowd of well-wishers who were still applauding. Over a hundred and fifty police officers were in attendance to wish their friend and leader goodbye. Greg had refused to attend the ceremony, complaining he was too weak. But Mayor Harkin insisted and after the encouragement of several of Greg's friends, he agreed to attend the celebration.

It was hot for an October day in Miami Beach. The temporary aluminum stage, set up in front of City Hall for the occasion, reflected the sun into Greg's eyes and the baseball cap he wore didn't help the glare that burned his eyes and made him squint. His police uniform fit him like a large sack, but Maggie had pulled the surplus material around his back in an attempt to make a better appearance. Greg focused his eyes on the World War II cannon mounted in the courtyard, its barrel pointed south toward the police building. He tried to remember what had gotten him to this point. He remembered very little about the shooting but recalled the approaching sirens and someone asking, "Is the captain dead?"

Mitch Hammond, his wife and two children, stepped to the podium. Mitch reached down to touch the shoulder of the man he had saved. Greg was startled by Mitch's touch and his body jerked in the wheelchair.

Maggie leaned forward and pulled Mayor Harkin from the microphone. "Please make this quick. I must get him out of here. He's too sick to be here."

"I understand, Maggie, hang in there with us for just a little longer," the mayor whispered.

Bill Riley, standing with other plain-clothes officers from the Narcotics Unit, walked into the crowd and approached an elderly man using an umbrella to keep the sun off his bald head.

"Excuse me, the captain needs your help."

He reached out for the umbrella and snatched it from the shocked man's hand. Bill walked toward the stage and presented the umbrella to Maggie who smiled a thank-you to him. She opened the umbrella to shade her husband. Riley looked back toward the elderly man and winked, gesturing a thumbs up. The old man hesitated, then smiled, nodding his approval.

Fifteen minutes passed and Mayor Harkin was on his typical political roll. It was apparent he didn't intend to keep his remarks short and Maggie could smell that Greg's colostomy bag was overflowing. She closed the umbrella and laid it on the awards table just behind the podium. Without speaking, she turned the wheelchair toward the back stairs.

Riley saw what was happening and grabbed two officers for assistance in getting Captain Strong's wheelchair off the stage.

Mayor Harkin turned to see Maggie and her husband leaving but continued to speak, not missing a word, keeping his composure, always the perfect politician. Several officers helped Maggie get the wheelchair down the steps.

"Where's your car, Maggie?" Riley asked.

Maggie rushed to the curb, and then turned to speak to Riley.

"The son-of-a-bitch is more interested in his damn glory than my husband's health. I should've never brought him here. This is my fault. Look at him, Bill. You've known Greg for years, look at him." Maggie's eyes filled with tears.

"The car, Maggie, where's the car?" Bill asked again. Maggie pointed to the shiny, black 1972 Oldsmobile parked at the curb a short walk from where they stood. As the officers loaded their captain into the car, they heard the Mayor continue.

"And so it is my privilege to present this award to Mitch Hammond, our Miami Beach Citizen of the Year. Mitch, your wife and children must be very proud of you today for you're an inspiration to us all. You have gone far beyond what anyone would expect from a law abiding citizen. Saving one of our finest from the jaws of death is the ultimate contribution that any citizen could give. It is also my..."

Riley slammed the door to the Olds, shutting off the outside world. Maggie pulled away from the curb and raced down Washington Avenue, speeding in front of hundreds of officers. Out of the corner of her eye, she spotted Greg's friend, Pete Spoto, standing at the rear of the crowd. Maggie licked her lips and tasted her salty tears. She screamed out at a crowd of well-wishers who couldn't hear her words. "We are done, people...we are done. Greg, listen to me, baby, we are done!" The car continued speeding south on Washington Avenue until it was out of sight.

Bill Riley stood at the curb with his hands in his pockets, then turned to a friend. "This is the end of a great era for this department. There'll never be another Greg Strong."

CHAPTER FIVE

ONE YEAR LATER

Maggie stood naked in front of her full-length mirror in the large dimly lit bedroom of her North Carolina mountain home. Staring at her body, she placed her hands on her large round breasts and fondled her nipples, causing each to rise in personal excitement. She made note of her small waist and flat stomach. Sliding her hands down to her waist, she felt her smooth and contoured mid section. Maggie smiled, dropping her hands to her side. *Not bad for an old broad*, she thought as she turned sideways to see a profile of her tiny, well formed body.

She had picked up her mirror watching habit from her husband who used it when he was a policeman. It's how he mentally and physically kept in shape for all those years. He would stare at his naked body for at least ten minutes each week, making note of any imperfections. There were few.

The hips, she muttered to herself, *got to work on the hips*. She turned to face her husband, sleeping in their bed. It had been just over a year since the shooting. She studied her husband's breathing as a mother checks the breathing of her newborn infant. She slipped on one of his old dress shirts and buttoned the front. Pulling her pony tail band from her long blond hair, she dropped her arms, allowing the sleeves of the shirt to fall inches below the ends of her fingers, making her appear more tiny than she was. "Give up on the hips," Greg would tell her, "It's hereditary. Nothing you can do about it."

She moved to the foot of the bed and looked down at the man she loved. *God, he's just a shadow of what he used to be*, she thought as she knelt at the foot of their bed to give Duke, their nine year old German shepherd, a few pats and a hug goodnight. Duke would remain at the foot of their bed all night, not moving until Greg woke in the morning. More than just a loyal pet, he had always been closer to Greg than Maggie. Since Greg's retirement, the two were inseparable.

Maggie turned out the remaining light and climbed into bed. The bedroom was engulfed in darkness. It was a cloud covered night and since there were no neighbors or street lights for miles, the only light in the room was provided by the clock that sat on her bed table. As she watched the second hand turn, she tried to wash her mind of all her thoughts so she could join her husband in sleep. The katydids seemed nosier than usual. Maggie wondered whether the overcast evening was the reason. Their racket filled the bedroom and she knew she was going to have another restless night.

Her thoughts turned to the assassination attempt on her husband. She remembered the two uniformed officers who picked her up at the airfield where she worked and drove her to the hospital. On the way she had overheard an announcement over the police radio that her husband was dead. The radio was turned off but it was too late. When she arrived in the emergency room, the chief of police held her and told her that Greg was the best police officer the department had ever had. She remembered he had said the same exact thing to another wife a year earlier after the department lost an officer in a bank robbery. With the knowledge that her husband was dead, she pushed herself from the chief's arms to turn and cry but was confronted by the mayor who was rushing toward her, wiping tears from his eyes.

Oh God, another phony, lying politician, she thought to herself as she braced herself for his hug. "Maggie, Maggie, I'll never forget Captain Strong as long as I live," the mayor had said.

What a joke, she thought, remembering how much Greg hated Mayor Harkin and his corrupt organization. He pulled Maggie close and hugged her. She stood there tolerating his hug with her arms to her side as he held her.

Thinking about the unpleasantness of that encounter made Maggie remember the firefighter standing at the end of the corridor and how she rushed to him for answers about her husband's death. That was when she learned her husband may not be dead, but was hanging on by a single thread of life. The firefighter had told her the thing keeping Greg alive was a cellophane wrapper from a pack of Marlboro cigarettes which he had shoved deep into the lung puncture in his chest. He had held the wrapper in place as Greg was being loaded onto the gurney. He continued to hold it in place with two fingers until doctors at the hospital could seal the wound better.

In an effort to not re-live the memory of the shooting for the hundredth time, Maggie turned in the bed to face her husband's back. She snuggled next to him and kissed his back. She ran her left arm around his body, feeling the long scar on his stomach. Maggie pulled herself closer, entwining her arm with his. She was reminded he had lost over forty pounds and had gained little of it back. He was as weak as she had ever seen him and it seemed as if he wasn't getting any stronger. The colostomy opening in his side had taken twice as long to heal than was normal, but the doctors tried to put a happy face on Greg's physical condition.

Sex was something they didn't even talk about anymore. She had once mentioned it to Greg's surgeon. He laughed saying, "The man lost twelve feet of intestine, a quarter of his lung and a piece of his finger. He's getting better. Just give him time."

That was eight months ago and Greg didn't seem to be improving. Maggie worried as much for her husband's psychological health as for his physical well being. He was once one of the strongest men on the force. Now he could no longer climb the stairs from the driveway to their kitchen carrying grocery bags without resting midway. He would get angry at himself, and then lie in bed for hours, staring at nothing.

***

Maggie didn't realize she had fallen into a deep sleep until Greg sat up in bed with a jolt, startling her. Maggie reached out for him, "It's okay, just another dream."

"Shush, listen," Greg responded. Maggie sat up in bed

next to him and that's when she heard Duke's deep, soft growl. The katydids were now silent, meaning it was after 3 AM. Maggie reached out to touch her husband's bare shoulder. He had broken into a cold, clammy sweat. He twitched, startled by her touch.

"Let's initiate the plan," Greg whispered.

"No, honey, it's just the bear again. Let's check it out first." Greg snapped his fingers. Duke quieted and stood at the closed bedroom door, tail motionless, ready for action.

"No, Maggie, first we'll initiate the plan and then I'll check it out." Maggie and Greg could now hear the crunching of car tires on the long gravel driveway to their home. Headlights lit up the bedroom as the car swung into the driveway at the front of the house. Greg pulled his .44 caliber magnum from its place at the side of the bed. Maggie put on her robe, pulled Greg's old light-weight five shot revolver from her bed table and headed for the basement in darkness.

They had practiced the exercise so many times. Maggie moved with the efficiency of a blind person in familiar surroundings. Once in the basement, she entered the unfinished cellar from a downstairs bedroom closet, crawling through a well hidden cubby hole behind a rack of hanging clothes. Positioning herself behind the heat pump air handler, big enough to hide two people, she sat on a portable camp chair placed there earlier. Maggie had a clear shot of anyone entering the cellar through the small crawl space. In total darkness, she groped for the flashlight sitting on top of the air handler. It would be turned on when needed.

Maggie was confident in her shooting abilities. She

would sometimes attend practice with her husband and shoot with the best of the SWAT team. The officers joked with her, calling her "Dead Eye Maggie." The last time her heart had pounded this hard, the suspect intruder turned out to be a bear tearing down their three bird feeders. But this was different, she thought. *Bears don't drive cars.* She was worried for Greg's safety and prayed he would have the strength to handle whatever was coming. She thought, *Who in the hell would come here at this time of the morning?*

Now that she was in position, she turned on her flashlight, lifted the receiver of the small phone Greg had installed near the heating unit and dialed the seven digit police department phone number. She had been taught well by her husband how to report emergencies to small town police departments.

"Cypress Police Department, is this an emergency?"

"Yes, it is. We have an intruder inside the house. Please listen carefully: 21 Meadow Wood in Cypress." She repeated the address and hung up, not waiting for a response. Then she took the phone off the hook so the police couldn't call back. She knew that unless she created an atmosphere of urgency, small town officers go to calls when they're good and ready. She was confident they would dispatch a marked unit right away.

While Maggie sat poised, listening for any sound, Greg positioned himself in the dining room and pulled the bullet-proof vest over his head and fastened the Velcro straps tight until he had trouble breathing. The vest had been given to him at his retirement party as a gag gift. He looked out the side window of the dining room, using a small mirror attached to the end of a two foot pole. Motion detectors had illuminated the entire front of the house. A brand new black Cadillac Fleetwood sat in the driveway, engine running and headlights on. The car's tinted windows were as dark as the paint, but Greg could see through the front windshield there was only one person in the front seat. Seconds seemed like minutes. Nothing happened. Greg spotted the flashing lights of a uniformed squad car in the distance. Relief poured over him. Once the police unit was close, the mystery intruder turned off the Caddy's engine, opened the driver's door, lighting up its interior, and exited with his hands over his head.

Since Greg couldn't identify the man, he decided to stay put. The intruder walked from his car and faced the arriving police car, giving the officer a clear view of his entire body. Gun drawn, the officer ordered the man to the prone position with his arms outstretched on the gravel driveway.

What the hell is going on, Strong thought? *This guy waited for the police and then anticipated their commands.* He then turned to Duke and gave the order, "Leave it." Duke's ears lay back for just an instant and his tail began to wag in anticipation of meeting those in front of the house. Greg raced to the basement to tell Maggie it was safe for her to come out.

After searching the man, the officer allowed him to rise to his feet, but ordered he keep his hands behind his head. In less than a minute Greg and Maggie walked from their house to the front of the Cadillac.

"You know this man, Captain?" The officer swung the man around for them to see. Greg and Maggie stared in shock.

Maggie put both hands to her mouth and spoke under her breath. "Oh God...no! How can this be?"

Greg put his arm around Maggie and pulled her close. The intruder dropped one hand from behind his head and put a finger to his lips and spoke.

"Shh", he whispered and smiled at both of them. There was an uncomfortable pause as the three stood staring.

Breaking the silence, the officer spoke, "Captain, it's obvious from the look on your face you know this man. Is he a friend?"

"He's a friend, Officer Hudson. He's an old friend. He looks like Pete Spoto...I think." Greg spoke without looking at the officer, unable to take his eyes off the intruder. He couldn't believe what he was seeing. The two men moved toward each other and embraced. "I thought you were dead, you son-of-a-bitch. Whose damn funeral did Maggie and I attend?"

"Sorry about the dramatic entrance. I knew you wouldn't let me near the house without a police check. We'll talk. Get rid of the officer," Spoto whispered. Greg pulled away and turned toward the policeman.

"Emery, can we list this call as unfounded, no intruder, and no one on the premises?"

"Not a problem, Captain, good night...or good morning...whatever. Almost quittin' time for me," he smiled. "Good evening Captain; Mrs. Strong."

The officer waved as he circled the driveway and disappeared down the long gravel road. Pete stood watching the officer and once he was out of sight he turned to face his friends. "That's it? No report? No nothing? Just a wave goodbye?"

Greg laughed, "Welcome to Cypress, North Carolina, and the simple life. It took some time for me to adjust to this life but now I'm on their clock. It's nice. You get used to it."

"Maggie, you look more beautiful than I ever remember. How do you manage to stay so young looking?" Pete asked.

Maggie didn't smile or respond to Pete's compliment but turned and walked into the house, arms folded around her robe.

"Come on in, Pete, I'll fix you a scotch," Greg offered.

Pete smiled, "No scotch for me, I've been on the wagon for over a year now, since the automobile accident. Name's not Pete anymore either. I'm now Mario. I always wanted to be a Mario. I always hated Peter. It's like something you keep in your pants. Mario is a fine name. It sounds like I own a restaurant and you know how much I like to cook."

Duke and the two men walked into the house and found Maggie in the kitchen making coffee.

Greg and Maggie had attended Pete's funeral over six months ago in Miami. He had reportedly been killed in the line of duty during an assignment in Panama right after his visit with President Nixon. The funeral was huge, befitting a man of Pete's reputation. Even Director Levinson, who hated Pete's guts, flew in and said glowing things about Pete's work. Over three thousand law enforcement personnel had attended the funeral, coming from all over the world. The funeral procession to the cemetery was so long that the lead hearse had arrived at the gravesite before the last car left the church grounds, twenty one miles away. It was a major event, closing a huge portion of I-95 with roadblocks everywhere. It was all about honoring a man that Greg Strong admired and respected.

"I'll ask you again. Whose funeral did we attend?"

Pete smiled. "I forgot his name, some wino they had frozen at the morgue, no relatives, and no next of kin. Even the funeral director didn't know who he buried. It was one of DEA's finer moments. I hate to admit this, but it was Levinson's idea. It was the way to make everything go away. As you know D.E.A. paid a bundle of money to the Knights, but my death put a real damper on the amount of the award. They would shit if they knew I was alive."

The two men sat, sipping from their coffee mugs in the Strongs' oversized country kitchen. Then Greg could hold it no longer. He began to chuckle, and then laugh, then louder and louder. Then Pete started laughing and the two were so loud, Duke became nervous and started to bark with concern. Maggie sat stone faced at the table watching her husband. It was the first time she had seen him laugh since the shooting. But she forced herself not to be a part of the festivities and restrained her emotions. She was a seasoned policeman's wife who feared the worst was about to happen.

"That whole ceremony...to bury a fucking homeless wino?" Greg laughed, holding the scar on his stomach.

"They also paid for my nose and chin job. I'm surprised you even recognized me. Don't I look different?" Pete held his head up so Maggie and Greg could see a profile.

Maggie stared at Pete as her mind raced. Pete was a man she didn't love or admire. It was Pete who talked her husband into taking an assignment in New York for a month of undercover work that almost got him killed. Pete Spoto was the federal agent who had encouraged her husband's drinking. It was he that Greg had spent night after night with, chasing down dealers and their ilk. Maggie felt Pete had stolen her husband away and that somehow his assassination attempt wouldn't have occurred if Greg had not been working with him. She blamed him for it all.

As her anger grew, she found she could no longer hold back her emotions so she blurted, "I would know you, you son-of-a-bitch, if they cut off your face and sewed on another. It's your mouth that gives you away, Pete...or Mario...or whoever you are... Why are you here? May I assume if you're supposed to be dead, you must be retired? Or is that assuming too much? Is this a social visit or have you come here to make my life miserable again?"

Pete reached out to Maggie, holding up his coffee cup. "Pour more coffee, Maggie, and let's sit here and talk. I'm not your enemy; never have been. Greg and I were in a nasty business together. You knew that. Your husband is the best police officer I've ever known. He's a sharpshooter, a tactical person who always nailed his man. Why do you think they called Greg 'The Predator'?"

Maggie was still full of emotion. Hoping not to embarrass the man she loved, she reached out and touched Greg's arm, "Take a damn good look at him and listen to what I'm about to tell you, Pete. He's a ghost of what he used to be and I don't think he's getting better. He's not a predator; he's the man I cherish, the man I want to keep alive. He has so damn

46

many enemies the homicide detectives didn't know where to look first after the shooting."

Pete could hear the anger in Maggie's voice.

Maggie continued. "The people who hired the assassination of my husband are still out there and I can't sleep because of that. You come in here, just like old times, like nothing has happened. I can't do it anymore. I'm no longer the brave woman I once was. Damn you for driving here in the middle of the night and scaring the shit out of me."

Maggie had started to cry, but she wouldn't wipe the tears from her face or take her eyes from Pete. She wanted him to see her emotion.

Pete pleaded with Maggie, "I'm not to blame for Greg's condition, Maggie, I had nothing to do with any of that."

While Pete Spoto may well have been the most ruthless, daring undercover agent DEA had ever experienced, he was also a man with deep personal feelings and convictions about loyalty, trust, and honor. Pete reached out to touch Maggie's hand but she pulled it away.

"You're here on a mission. I know you, Pete, here like this, no warning, wearing a new face. Well, we don't want any part of it, do we, Greg? We're done with that. Watch me say the words, Pete. We-are-done-with-you!"

Greg reached out to hold his wife's hand from across the table in the center of their kitchen. When he touched her she pulled away and burst into a full cry. All the pent-up stress, Pete Spoto's arrival, her taking care of Greg, wondering why he wasn't getting healthier, came pouring out at once. Greg jumped from his chair to hold his wife. He felt sorry for her, having to care for him and watch him like a child for the better part of a year. They never went anywhere or did anything. She was his nurse. All he could think to do was hold her until her crying started to subside.

Pete was also full of emotion and was surprised at Maggie's outburst. He didn't realize the extent of what she had been through. Without showing emotion himself, Pete reared back in his kitchen chair and held up his cup to toast Maggie. "Well then, 'Dead Eye', I've got good news for you. I'm done also; retired, finished with undercover work, no badge, no reports, no sleepless nights, it's over. But you've got to stop crying, Maggie, because it freaks me out that I made you cry."

Pete paused, hoping Maggie would stop, and then he continued. "Why do you think we had the funeral, Maggie? There are many cartel people who want me dead. DEA wanted me to go away and it was time for me to retire anyway. Levinson presented DEA with the funeral idea and they bit on it. The lawyers who think I'm dead said it took about two million off the final judgment on the lawsuit. The plastic surgery on the kid's eyelid didn't go well and the lawyers wanted a five million dollar judgment just for that."

Maggie looked at Pete with skepticism. "How does Katy feel about all of this?"

"Katy is gone. She divorced me right after the accident. She couldn't handle the embarrassment anymore. She hated Panama from my last assignment and vowed never to return. Besides, now she thinks I'm dead. She's living with an accountant, nine to five guy who reminds me of Mr. Peepers."

Maggie was beginning to gain back some control of

herself. She rationalized she could cope with a retired Pete Spoto. She wiped the tears from her face and managed a smile at Pete, trying to think positive and convince herself this was just a social visit.

The three sat at the kitchen table well into mid-morning, discussing old friends, assignments and the good times they had together. Maggie lowered her emotional shields further and allowed herself to remember that Pete was a funny, easy-going friend. Pete was astounded that neither Maggie nor Greg had brought up the Nixon visit and he guessed they were afraid to ask.

Pete excused himself to use the bathroom but, instead walked out the front door and entered his car. Unlocking his glove compartment, he pulled out a tightly wrapped paper bag and sat it in his lap. Then he removed a 9 mm automatic pistol from its holster and shoved it into his waist band, hiding it with his shirt. Entering the house, Pete threw the bag, sealed with tape, on the kitchen table.

"Go ahead, Greg, open it," Pete said.

Greg and Maggie smiled at each other, wanting to believe this was just a gift, a present from an old friend they had not seen for a year. Because the bag was so well sealed, Greg pulled a kitchen knife from a drawer and began to cut open the bag. Greg and Maggie stared at the contents, then at Pete.

"What the hell is this?" Greg asked.

Pete smiled, "I know you want to hear about my real visit with President Nixon and not the fake one. So let me tell you."

Greg's anger showed in his face. "Wrong, I don't give a

damn about the president. I want to know what this is." Greg held up the bundled package of one hundred dollar bills, held together with three large rubber bands.

"Oh that, it's $200,000 of non-sequenced old bills, none of which are registered with DEA, or anyone else for that matter; my gift to you from an old friend."

The two men stared at each other without blinking. Maggie rose to get more coffee. She shook her head, muttering to herself, "I knew it, I just knew it."

While Maggie still had her back turned, Pete pulled the 9 mm pistol from his waist and pointed it at his old friend. Greg sat expressionless, knowing that Pete would never shoot him. Pete smiled and slid the gun across the table.

"It's not loaded. It's my other gift to you. No registration, no serial numbers and brand new. The rifling has been removed from the barrel, making it as clean as a rookie's locker. In the handle are four firing pins, polished by a German craftsman who is a personal friend of mind. The suppressor is on order and should be in your hands next week."

"Get out of my house, Pete. Get out," Maggie shouted, hurling her full cup of coffee at him. By the time the cup hit the table, most of the hot coffee had spilled across the kitchen floor. Pete put his hand out and caught the cup as it slid across the table toward him.

"Nice throw, Maggie! I'll leave as you wish. All I ask is another ten minutes of your time. Sit here for just ten minutes and then I'll get up and walk away and, if you wish, never see you again. Is that fair, Maggie?"

"Nothing is ever fair when you're involved, Pete. I don't believe you."

Greg reached out for his wife as she approached him to be comforted. "Maggie, there's nothing to worry about here. I'm all right. Let's hear Pete out. There's no harm in just listening. Pete is our friend, Maggie. Have you forgotten how many meals you have cooked for this man, how much fun we've had together? Doesn't he deserve another ten minutes?"

Greg slid the bundle of money and the weapon back in front of Pete, hoping to appease his wife. "You've got ten minutes, then out of respect for Maggie, I want you to leave."

Maggie stood silent, staring at the two men. Her silence signaled her husband she would allow Pete to continue.

"Good enough, Greg. I promise. Maggie, please sit down." Pete smiled at her as she sat, but Maggie wouldn't look at him, keeping her arms folded in a defiant position.

Pete began to tell the story of his meeting with President Nixon. He told Greg and Maggie how, after the small, private award ceremony in the Oval Office, Nixon ordered everyone to leave except him. Once alone, Nixon walked up to Pete and hugged him. Pete was startled and embarrassed by this, but did nothing. Then Nixon whispered into Pete's ear, *"I think you're the toughest son-of-a-bitch I've ever met."* Then Nixon released his grip on Pete.

Still shocked by the hug, Pete stammered, "Thank you, Mr. President."

The president smiled, gesturing toward a chair. "Sit down, Agent Spoto, let's talk."

Nixon chose not to sit at his desk but picked one of the chairs facing the large bullet proof windows behind his desk. Nixon explained how one of his major goals was to stop drug trafficking into the country. He also told Pete how frustrated he was at not being unable to accomplish more, even though billions had been poured into the effort.

"What the hell are we doing wrong?" the president had asked Pete. "They're kicking our asses and we can't stop them. You're a street-tough narcotics agent who has seen it all. I've read your file, reviewed your work and, by the way, I know about the ugly incident in Miami when you shot your informant; most unfortunate. I also know about the automobile accident with Evelyn Knight and her daughter. Did you know Robert Knight is my neighbor on Key Biscayne?"

Nixon didn't wait for an answer. "With me, you can relax on all that. I don't care about small shit. Let's look at the big picture. I always like to look at the big picture."

Nixon got up from his chair and walked to a small table on the far side of the Oval Office. Opening a drawer, he reached in and pulled out two cigars. "Could I interest you in a cigar? They're pretty good, not Cuban, but still good." Nixon walked back to his chair, handed one to Pete and presented a lighter. "Here, I'll let you light your own. It's bad luck to light another man's cigar."

The two men lit their cigars and blew smoke at each other.

"So where was I? Oh yeah, what are we doing wrong? Tell me how to better impact illegal trafficking? I need information from the street level."

Pete sat silent for a moment to read the expressions on

Greg and Maggie's faces, then he responded. "I was in disbelief. I thought, here I am, a twelve step member, a drunk and a divorcee, smoking cigars with the president of the United States and being asked for advice on US policy toward drug trafficking."

Greg was intrigued with Pete's story but Maggie pretended not to care. She found it preposterous the leader of the strongest nation in the world would ask a man who was probably the most dangerous man in the country for advice. Both Maggie and Greg had been close enough to federal law enforcement work to have heard stories about how unorthodox Nixon could be at times.

"What did you tell him, Pete?" Greg asked.

"Can't tell you, old friend, I promised you ten minutes and I only have four left. I couldn't possibly finish in that length of time." Pete smiled, looking at Maggie.

Silence set in again as Maggie contemplated her move. After a long pause, she spoke with a disgusted tone. "Go ahead, Pete, you always get your way. Who am I to stop you? I never could anyway, so go ahead. What the hell did you tell Nixon? There, I'm asking."

"Thanks, Maggie, you won't regret this."

Maggie chuckled, "Yes, I will, Pete, yes, I will."

Pete leaned forward in his chair and slid the money and weapon into the center of the table, into an invisible no man's land. He smiled at Maggie and spoke. "I told him the truth. Criminals, especially drug dealers, never play by the rules. Drug agents, on the other hand, are restricted by politics, laws and liberal court rulings that handcuff them so they can't do their job. The dealers work around the clock at their trade. Drug agents work five days a week with occasional overtime. We go on vacation with our families, have sick time, sit in court for days on cases while they smuggle dope into the country around the clock. We play by the rules; they don't have any rules."

Pete got up from his chair to get another cup of coffee before continuing. "Then I asked the president how he expected to win under those conditions. I told him he should be amazed that we do as well as we do under the circumstances."

Greg stood, grabbed his empty coffee cup and walked to get a refill. "I'll bet old sourpuss wasn't too happy to hear that. How did he react?" Greg asked.

"Well, first he got political with me, telling me that democracy is not cheap, that there is a price to pay for freedom and all that bull-shit we've heard a thousand times. Then he asked me what if we didn't have to play by the rules. If we could play by their rules, which are no rules, would it make a difference?"

Greg had returned to his seat. Maggie felt the loving, reassuring stroke of his hand on her hair as he sat. She gave him a quick smile and turned to look back at Pete. He had her attention. She was feeling such mixed emotions. Pete was such a likable man, so dedicated to his work, but the craziest man she had ever known, so smart and so wild at the same time. This combination made him a person who was capable of any possible behavior. She trusted his loyalty to her husband but always feared he would get Greg killed.

"You've changed, Maggie. What's troubling you?" Pete asked.

She shook her head.

"Nothing, Pete; just nothing."

While she was intrigued with Pete's story, she feared where it was heading. She was also beginning to feel a little guilty about the terrible way she had treated Pete since his arrival at their home. After all, Greg was right; they had been close friends for many years. Her emotions were in turmoil. She reached out to touch Pete's hands, folded on the table, surprising him.

"Bottom line, Pete, where are you going with this?" Maggie asked.

Pete smiled, pushing the gun and bundle of money back in front of Greg. "Now that's the Maggie I know and love. Cut to the chase, a no bullshit girl. Bottom line; how's this for a bottom line? A month after my visit with Nixon, I met a guy in Panama named Halderman. He's a personal friend of Nixon and his chief of staff. A real nice guy. After my visit with him, I no longer have to play by the rules. No reports, no bosses, no courts, no testifying, unlimited expense accounts and two hundred grand for each of my team members with a one year contract and an option to re-up for another year if we're successful."

Pete hesitated, staring at Greg and Maggie, giving them time to digest what he had told them.

"This is about four people working together, doing what we do best, killing scumbag cartel people with the blessings of the government...better still, the president. So I retired, had the funeral, got a face job and presto, here I am in your kitchen ready to go."

Almost afraid to ask the next logical question in fear of

showing too much interest, Maggie contemplated her next move.

"Tell me about the 'we' part. Who are the others? I know you want Greg. Why else would you be here, but who are the other two?"

Pete sat silent so Greg and Maggie could digest all they had been told. Just as Pete was going to speak, Greg reached out and slid the money and gun back in front of Pete and shook his head.

Pete looked surprised. "You should at least hear the details before making that decision."

Maggie wrapped her arm around her husband's arm and spoke. "No, Pete, Greg made a good decision. This is not the old Greg Strong you think you know. He takes a nap, sometimes twice a day, not because he likes to but because he has to. He's retired, retired, not like you. You'll go to your grave involved with dope. It's your life, but not ours, not anymore. We are isolated up here in these mountains, out of fear, but it's good to get away from all the ugliness of the city. We don't need the money or the aggravation."

"I got Riley," Pete blurted out... "I got Bill Riley," he repeated, hoping to further his cause.

Greg couldn't believe what Pete was saying. After Greg's retirement, Sergeant Riley had been fired from the police department for using cocaine on duty. The drug use had been occurring for some time and Greg knew it. One night, Greg and Bill got into a violent fist fight over Riley's use of cocaine and Riley found himself no match for his stronger opponent. Later, Riley was kicked out of the unit and returned to the uniform patrol division. The rat squad found enough dope in his locker to charge him with possession with intent to sell. He beat the charges in court on a technicality but couldn't keep his job. Riley was last seen by Greg and Maggie tending bar in a poor section of Fort Lauderdale. Riley's wife had hung in with him out of loyalty.

Pete smiled at Greg and laughed at his surprised look.

"How about that for a team? Are we not the scariest three people on this planet?"

Pete knew, in spite of their disagreements, Greg still liked Riley and thought he was one of the most loyal and daring narcotics officers on the force.

"And the fourth?" Maggie asked, showing increased interest. "Who's the fourth?"

Pete leaned forward, pushing the money and weapon toward Maggie. "We need a pilot. Do you know a pilot we can trust, Maggie?"

"You gotta be kidding. You want me to fly for you so you can run around killing dope dealers? I'm not a cop, never wanted to be one. No, I'm not your pilot. Find someone else."

Pete tried to reassure her. "You don't even have to carry a gun, Maggie. We need a pilot we can trust. You're the best pilot I know. Just take us from point A to point B, that's all we need from you. You wind up making two hundred grand, plus Greg's two hundred grand. That will buy a lot of dog bones for Duke. The best part is you won't be away from Greg like it was in the old days when he worked. Think hard on this, Maggie. You don't have to give me an answer now. You and Greg have a lot to talk over. Don't let this be an emotional decision. Make it a business decision."

Maggie pushed the money back toward Pete. "We have nothing to talk over. I want you to leave. Leave now."

Without responding, Pete pushed back his chair and walked from the kitchen, leaving the money and the weapon on the kitchen table.

Pete turned and asked, "Are you going to walk me to my car? After all, we may never see each other again."

Maggie smiled, "Knowing you, I doubt that." Greg and Maggie followed Pete to his car.

Pete, watching Duke follow them out the front door, looked toward Greg and asked, "How old is Duke now? Do you still train with him at K9 School?"

"He just turned nine and retired with me. You knew we never used him on the job. I paid for his training and he was never owned by the city."

Getting into his Cadillac, Pete surprised Greg and Maggie once again. "I was going to wait for your answer before telling you this, but now I'm concerned you're not going to take my offer. Our first target will be the man who contracted your hit. How would you like to take out the guy who tried to have you killed?"

Pete was toying with Greg's mind. He reached for the electric window button and it began to close. Greg reached out and stopped the window from closing.

"That's bullshit. No one knows who hired that Canadian," Greg blurted out in anger. "He was an amateur with terminal cancer who did it for his ailing mother. That's all they found. What the hell do you have?"

Pete pushed his car door open and turned his body, placing both feet in the driveway.

"Listen to what I'm saying, Greg. I know...and you know the hit man had a brother. That brother got shit-faced in a Montreal bar and talked too much to the bartender. What he didn't know was the bartender also happens to be a DEA snitch. I found out about this when the bartender called DEA looking for money."

Greg dropped to one knee in his driveway to be at eye level with his friend. He grabbed Pete's shirt and wadded it into his fist.

"I swear to God, Pete, I'll beat the living shit out of you if you're lying to get me to come on board. Now look me in the eye and swear you're not lying."

"Lighten up, old friend. Let me finish the story," Pete said as he pulled Greg's hand from his shirt. "Anyway, don't forget you've lost your ability to carry through on that threat. Now be cool and let me finish." Pete brushed his shirt and collar with his hand, straightening it as best he could. Pete continued. "The hit man's brother told our snitch he met a guy with a lot of money who wanted a Miami cop taken down. Turns out you know the guy. The brother had no stomach for that kind of thing so he put him onto his brother who was dying of cancer with not much time to live anyway."

"Who's the guy, Pete? Why are you holding back? Who is this scumbag? And what the hell is the motive to have me hit?"

"Maybe you should sit down next to me on the passenger's side, Greg, because you're going to keel over when you hear the rest."

"I don't need to sit down, Pete. Why are you stalling? Finish the story."

"Okay, okay, the guy went on to tell the bartender the motive was personal. The guy's kid knocked up their seventeen year old Costa Rican housekeeper and was in serious trouble, getting shook down for big money. He was in Montreal looking for someone to take the contract. Does any of this light your torch, Greg?"

"Mayor Harkin? Are you talking about Mayor Harkin? I never blackmailed Harkin. I wanted him in jail for murdering his housekeeper. He put out the hit? What proof do you have?"

Pete pulled in his feet and closed the car door with the driver's window half up. "The housekeeper was blackmailing him, not you. And if you're looking for a smoking gun, I don't have it. I know Harkin withdrew thirty grand from a Cayman account two weeks before the Canadian tried to kill you. I also know from the Canadian's mother, her son gave her thirty grand in American money shortly thereafter, just before he headed for Miami. I also know Harkin hates your guts because you were in his face on a lot of shit he was working. If you squeeze Harkin, he'll squeal like a pig. He has no balls. Before you kill him, you'll know for sure."

CHAPTER SIX

Out of the corner of her eye, Maggie caught a glimpse of Duke's wagging tail as she walked from her bathroom with a toothbrush stuck in the side of her mouth. To her amazement, Duke was standing, staring at his sleeping master, watching him. Duke's tail moved, not in excitement, but with purpose. It seemed to Maggie as if Duke knew Greg had experienced a real good day.

Maggie kneeled next to Duke and whispered, "I love him, too, big boy." Duke became preoccupied with the toothbrush sticking out of the corner of Maggie's mouth and attempted to lick her face.

"Yuck, you have bad breath, go brush your teeth." Maggie returned to the bathroom to prepare for bed.

Duke was right, she thought. This had been Greg's very best day since the shooting. She had never seen him laugh so hard and for so long. He had been in good spirits since Pete, or Mario, as he wanted to be called, had come back into their lives in a most positive way. This rough and tumble, scary man, capable of killing in a flash, had done more for her husband in one visit than all the doctors and psychiatrists combined had accomplished in a year. For that, she was grateful.

She longed for Pete to return soon, but wished he had not dumped such a heavy decision on them. She sensed that Greg wanted to join the team even though he had not said so. The news that Pete had given them just before leaving was exciting. It had been on their minds for the remainder of the day, yet neither of them had spoken of it. It was just too much information, too fast and too soon, for them to digest. While Maggie disapproved of violence, she understood the need for it in the real world. She could pull the trigger on the man who had ordered Greg's murder and now she would have the opportunity to be a part of avenging her husband's assassination attempt.

The evening rain had silenced most of the outside noises of the forest except for the croaking of frogs on Watson Pond a half mile away. The bedroom had filled with dampness from the cool, late August evening rain so Maggie pulled the window shut, silencing the frogs and the rain. She took one last long look at her husband before turning off the small lamp next to the bed. He had missed both naps and had crashed into a deep sleep by seven o'clock. Maggie glanced at the small illuminated numbers on the clock in the dark bedroom. She hadn't gone to bed before eleven for over a year but she felt exhausted from her busy and eventful day. She knew it would be easy for her to sleep this night.

***

Maggie woke to the touch of her husband's lips on her

back just below her neck. Morning dawn filled the room with just enough light for her to see. She strained to listen if the rain had stopped but couldn't be sure. Greg reached to pull her closer. He whispered into her ear, "I love you, Maggie, I love you."

Maggie turned in the bed to face her husband. "I love you too, baby; always have and always will."

Greg pulled Maggie closer, slipping his hand under the back of her shirt and running it up her silky back. Maggie's large breasts pushed against Greg's chest and her nipples hardened with excitement. She reached up and unbuttoned the front of her shirt with the skill of a seasoned lover. Her exposed breasts now pressed against Greg's hairy chest. She wrapped a leg around his waist, pushing her pelvis forward and felt, for the first time in over a year, her husband was erect. They kissed passionately. She had not had sex since the shooting. Masturbation was disappointing and not fulfilling for her, so she had decided long ago to just do without and tried to avoid those things that would arouse her.

"I want to make love to you, Maggie," Greg whispered into her ear.

"Oh yes, honey, yes, I've missed you in my arms," Maggie answered.

She was wet in anticipation of what was about to occur. Without moving from their sides, Greg slowly entered her. Maggie gasped in excitement and wrapped both arms around his head, shoving her pelvis forward so she could feel her husband penetrate her more deeply. It had been so long since she had experienced this kind of pleasure. She pushed Greg onto his back while still clinging to him. Then she sat up on top of him, allowing him to fully enter her. Without moving, Maggie moaned. Her orgasm was amazing and long lasting. She could feel Greg's orgasm as his penis throbbed deep inside her. Greg and Maggie clung to each other, wrapped in each other's arms. After a moment of silence, Maggie pushed her face away from Greg's shoulder and smiled.

"My, my, we have to have Pete over more often."

Greg laughed and said, "That has to be the shortest sex we've ever had." Then he reached up and pulled her head back onto his shoulder and the two drifted back to sleep as the morning wore on.

***

Maggie woke and sensed Greg was missing from their bed. She turned to find she was right. She couldn't believe her eyes when she turned to face the clock and it read 10:12 AM. She jumped from the bed with concern and found Greg standing at the kitchen counter with coffee cup in hand.

"Maggie, I can't find those pills Doc Grossman gave me last year. Do you know where they are?"

Dr. Mark Grossman had not only been one of the physicians involved in Greg's recovery, he was also a friend. He had given Greg several bottles of protein drink and energy capsules to take daily, but Greg gave away the protein drink and never took the capsules. At the time, he was in such a state of depression he didn't want to get better.

"I put them away. They're in a bottom drawer in the bedroom. I'll get them," Maggie answered.

When Maggie returned with the capsules, she found

Greg sitting at the kitchen table dismantling the 9 mm weapon Pete had left behind. Maggie leaned down to kiss him, then sat at the table and slid the bottles toward him.

"Take a look inside this barrel, Maggie. It's void of all striations and is as slick and polished as any I've ever seen. Also, I can't find how the silencer attaches to the barrel. It must be something new on the market. The serial numbers haven't been ground away, they never existed. The manufacturer never put serial numbers on this weapon and you know what that means. This is special order from the C.I.A. I don't know how Pete pulled that off."

Maggie got up to pour herself coffee and then pulled her chair very close to Greg's. She sat, put her arm around his shoulder and hesitated before speaking.

"How do you feel after our morning encounter?"

Greg smiled at his wife. "It's been a long time. You're still a great lover, Maggie. It was very special for me. I'm not sure what's happening with me. I seem to have new life and I know I'm not any better today than I was yesterday. It's strange."

Maggie sipped from her cup then kissed his shoulder. "It's psychological, baby. Pete has gotten you all fired up and your psyche has made you better. While I'm not sure I like where we're headed, I love that, overnight, you seem to be a new man. I'm also frightened."

"Let's talk, Maggie. Me first, okay?"

Maggie nodded.

"I've given Pete's proposal a lot of thought. Here's what I'm feeling." Greg paused, staring down at his cup, gathering his thoughts. "If you're not in on this, then I'll pass also. I want to do this, but not without you. If that son-of-a-bitch Harkin tried to have me killed, then I've little choice but to kill him. You and I have been through a lot together, Maggie. Harkin took away a big piece of our lives, I want to take him out and I want you with me."

Maggie could feel his energy flowing from him to her. *How could this be*, she thought? Was he always physically well but so psychologically defeated he lost all his energy? She couldn't understand what was happening to him and it scared her. Greg seemed alive again and she wanted to please him so much yet she realized the consequences of what they were about to do. After a moment of silence she spoke.

"There's more to this than just taking out Harkin. We'll be under contract to kill drug dealers. And if we're caught, do you think Nixon is going to get us out of this? He'll disown us and deny everything. We'll be hung out to dry and Pete's friend, Halderman, won't be found. Have you thought about that, Greg? And are we now ready to become government assassins just to make Nixon's drug stats look better? What are we becoming here?"

Greg frowned at his wife. "I don't give a damn about Nixon's drug stats, Maggie. I want to find out if Harkin tried to have me killed. If he did, I'll have no trouble in wasting him. Then we'll chase after a few minor cartel people for one year and quit. I promise, just one year. In the end, we'll be able to be free. We won't have to worry about every strange car that pulls into our driveway. We'll have $400,000 buried someplace and life will return to normal. Well, as normal as we have ever been. So what do you think, Maggie? Do we do this together or not at all?"

"Then the decision has been made, baby. I'm in this all the way." Maggie smiled to reassure her husband and to show she wasn't concerned whether she was making the right decision. "But promise me one thing. Speak with Riley about his mouth and manner. He's such a pig and I know, out of respect for you, he would refrain from being crude if you asked. If he can do that for me then this is what I would call a great team. I must also admit we are a scary bunch, to say the least."

Greg finished assembling the semi-automatic weapon Pete had given him. He checked the weapon for smooth operation, making sure the brass jacketed bullets passed from the magazine, up the ramp and into the chamber.

He looked at Maggie and smiled.

"Riley can be controlled and I'll speak to him as you asked. First, he's afraid of me and, second, he'll want to prove he's still worthwhile in spite of his prior cocaine habit. We'll see if he's still on the wagon. That's important."

Greg shoved the automatic into a worn, beat-up holster and walked toward a kitchen drawer. Pulling out a dozen of Maggie's recipes he slid the gun to the back of the drawer and placed the recipes on top. He turned to face Maggie.

"It's Pete I'm concerned about. Nobody controls that guy, which brings up the question of who is running this team. We never discussed who would call the shots when we're on a mission."

Maggie laughed, "You don't know the answer to that? You know Pete will want to make all the decisions, at least the important ones."

"I don't care, Maggie. Once I have my rendezvous with

Harkin, the rest is unimportant to me. I say let's find 'em, smoke 'em and head for the mountains when our year is up. Oh, not to change the subject, I'm going for a nap. Wanna join me?"

"You know if I go in there with you there'll be no napping. Nah, I'll plan dinner and you sleep. But we'll rendezvous in the bedroom after dark."

"Sounds like a plan to me. Don't let me sleep for more than an hour. We have a lot of plans to make and a lot to get ready."

CHAPTER SEVEN

TWO MONTHS LATER

The meeting lasted until 2 AM and everyone was mentally exhausted. Tomorrow would be the team's first full day of work. All the materials needed for the mission were in place. The research was complete and everything was going well.

Maggie tried to sleep but couldn't, her mind full of concern. She worried about the Watergate break-in but rationalized it had nothing to do with Nixon. *But what if he was involved,* she pondered. *How would that affect us if Nixon was involved?* She tried to dismiss these thoughts from her head.

Greg turned in his sleep to face her. She lay there, listening to the soft, shallow breathing of this man she loved so much. He had regained most of his weight back and he looked like the old, healthy Greg. He was alive again, driven by the desire to get revenge on the man who ordered his death.

They made love often and they exercised together every

day. Greg was now using the protein powders and special vitamins the doctors had recommended. Always hungry, he consumed everything in sight, but came down with intestinal attacks as a result of eating the junk food Riley and Spoto brought into their home. Maggie closed her eyes, smiling, and remembered an incident when Pete and Bill came to the house with a large bag of McDonald's burgers and fries. She had lost her temper and blurted in anger. "Stop bringing that goddamn shit into this house." She covered her mouth, not believing her language.

Then she recalled Riley's retort, "Please, watch your language around Pete." For the most part, Riley had kept his promise to keep his language and demeanor in check.

Maggie opened her eyes to have a last look at her husband. She thought, *I have my man back, not whole, but better than I've ever seen him since the shooting. What have I done to myself? I've joined with scary people to systematically commit murder.*

Her mind continued to wander. *I was once a good Catholic girl but now I'm driven by my intense love for this man. It's my love for him and my thirst for revenge that have brought me to this point. I justify what I'm about to do by telling myself this is a good thing. Eliminating some of the scum from this earth is not, after all, something that would be frowned upon by many of Greg's colleagues in law enforcement, if they should ever learn of this.*

Unable to sleep, her mind turned to Pete and his continuous pep talks. She knew Pete viewed her as the weakest link on the team and his speeches were convincing and intended to bolster the attitude that this was all a good thing. She went over his little speech time and time again.

Pete would say, "Soldiers are given awards and medals for killing people for our country. It's good to kill in wartime. War is nothing more than sanctioned killing by the government. If killing is sanctioned by the government, it's good, and that's all we're doing. We're at war for our government against drug smugglers and that makes everything all right."

Still, it was her conscience that wouldn't allow her to sleep. She knew if she asked Greg to quit the team, he would. Then she thought, *I'll not deprive him of this. He's whole again. I will, without hesitation, take an active role in murdering the Mayor of Miami Beach. Oh my God, this wasn't on my list of things to do when I graduated from Embry-Riddle flight school fifteen years ago. What is to become of me*, she thought? Fatigue conquered her and she drifted off to sleep.

***

Maggie woke, struggling out of a deep sleep. It was as if she had been drugged, but she knew it was the effects of exhaustion. Staring at the clock on her end table, she couldn't believe her eyes. It was just after eleven. Greg and Duke had left the bedroom and she could hear the grinding of the cement mixer in the back yard. Rushing to dress, she threw on yesterday's jeans and sweat shirt. She pulled open the blinds and bright North Carolina sun drenched the bedroom. After taking a quick look at the thermometer outside their window, she headed for the kitchen but found Greg sitting in the living room. Lying on the coffee table, next to Greg's coffee cup, was the CO-2 rifle he'd been practicing with for weeks.

"Hey, baby, how ya feelin' today?" Maggie asked as she leaned down to give Greg a kiss. "Why did you let me sleep so late?"

"I saw no need to wake you," Greg responded. "You're not needed this morning anyway so I let you sleep. Maggie, I'm one fired up old broken down retired police captain. This is our time. This is what we've waited for, what we've dreamed of since the shooting. Finding the son-of-a-bitch who ruined our lives and now it's our turn to ruin his. I know you're not totally on board with this, so I want to tell you how much I love you for joining me."

"Never doubt my love for you, Greg. I'm going for a cup of coffee. Want a refill?" Maggie responded, wanting to change the subject.

"Nah, I'm just finishing my third cup. You go ahead."

Greg followed his wife into the kitchen and stood, leaning against the country stove as he watched her fix her coffee. Maggie lifted her cup to her lips and took her first sip. Greg walked to the large kitchen window over the sink and Maggie joined him.

"It's thirty-eight friggin' degrees this morning. What do you figure it is in Miami, seventy or better?" Maggie asked.

"Don't know, but Pete is concerned about pouring cement in this weather. He says it affects the strength of the set, but I told him the contractors pour cement all the time in cold weather. But you know Pete, he contemplates every factor. Let's go see how it's going."

They slipped on wind breakers and walked out the back door to find Bill and Pete busy at work. Bill had just finished putting the last of four large casters on the bottom of the waxed cardboard box, pushing the long steel bolts through the bottom of the cardboard, causing them to protrude six inches into the box. The sides and bottom of the box had been reinforced with wood furring strips so it would hold the weight of the concrete.

"It's colder than a well digger's ass out here," Bill said as he spotted Maggie and Greg walking toward him. Maggie smiled. She knew it was Bill's way of saying good morning.

"And good morning to you, Bill", Maggie laughed.

"It's time, let's pour," Pete announced.

Bill and Pete tipped the barrel of the portable mixer, causing the mixed concrete to pour into the upright waxed box. The long steel caster bolts, protruding upright through the bottom of the box, disappeared, covered with cement. Once the cement filled the box, Pete pushed four stainless steel bolts into the wet cement, one for each corner. As everyone gathered around the box Pete measured the distance from each bolt.

"You know the old saying," Pete laughed. "Measure twice and cut once....or something like that. I want each of you to measure the distance between the bolts. If it's off more than a half inch, this won't work."

Pete watched his three team members take turns with the measurements, writing them on a small piece of paper. When the measurements were compared, everyone came up with the exact same numbers.

"There, that should do it. Is there still coffee?" Pete asked as the four entered the house. Pete poured his coffee as everyone settled in the living room.

Wanting to take immediate command, Pete ordered,

"Let's go over the plan once more, just to make sure we got the timing down."

Maggie looked at Pete with disgust. "No, damn it, how many times are we going to go over this? I'm sick of it. We've rehearsed this so often I'm dreaming about it. Enough is enough."

Riley responded. "I agree."

Greg added, "There is such a thing as over-planning. Is everyone straight on what has to be done? Does everyone know their job?"

The four sat silent, each making eye contact with the others, waiting for a response.

Pete broke the silence. "Okay, okay, we've planned enough. I'm going to clean the mixer. Anyone wanna help?" Pete asked. Greg raised his finger in acknowledgment and the two walked into the back yard.

Bill and Maggie were left staring at each other from across the living room.

"Scared, Maggie?" Riley asked.

"Damn right I'm scared. You've killed before. You can justify this in your mind anyway you want, but it's first degree murder no matter how you want to disguise it."

Riley shook his head, "Then get out now, Maggie, while there's still time because once you crank your engines and set your flaps, you're in this for good."

Maggie spoke in a harsh tone, "I'm already in this for good. I'm not wavering. Besides, I want to see that scumbag get what's coming to him. But there's no honor in this, so don't give me that speech about killing in war and all that crap. I don't want to hear it again." They sat glaring at each other.

Then Bill nodded in agreement and Maggie looked away, content she had gotten her point across.

Maggie rose from her chair. "I'm going to call for another weather update. I'm concerned about a small system drifting out of the Gulf into the Panhandle. I've got to keep an eye on that system. By dark it could be in our way."

"Why not file a damn flight plan?" Bill asked.

"No flight plan," Maggie raised her voice, "How many more times must I say that? This part of the mission is my call, not yours. If the weather is bad, we wait for another week. That's my call. You have no say. And furthermore".…. Bill raised his hands in surrender.

"Okay, okay, I forgot. We'll do it your way."

Pete and Greg walked in the back door, wet and cold from cleaning the mixer.

"You're not going to believe this but that hardening crap we put in the mixture is already working. It's been less than thirty minutes," Pete said, looking toward Bill,

"Told you not to worry," Bill laughed. "By show time, it will be as cured as it's going to get. Trust me on this."

"Trust you? If I didn't trust you, I wouldn't be here."

Later that afternoon, the three men struggled to load the hardened concrete block into the back of a rented panel truck. Using a four by eight-foot sheet of reinforced plywood for a ramp, they jacked the slab, sitting on casters, up the ramp using a come-a-long pulley.

"How much does that thing weigh?" Maggie asked as she watched the large block crawl up the ramp and into the back of the van.

"About two hundred pounds but that won't be a problem

later; you'll see," Pete responded, not taking his eyes off the slab.

Once the slab was in the truck, Pete locked the casters into place, securing the block just inside the back doors of the van. Then he turned and spoke. "Now we wait. I didn't sleep well last night. Bill kept me awake with his damn snoring so I'm going to sack out."

Pete walked into the house, pulled off his jacket and disappeared through a side door to his bedroom.

"I think we should all try to sleep. We need to be at our best for this, whadaya say?" Greg asked. Bill and Maggie nodded in agreement, although Maggie knew she wouldn't sleep. Napping wasn't her thing.

***

At 6:12 PM on November 1st, 1972, Maggie hung up the phone after receiving a final weather briefing while her three companions waited in anticipation.

"We're good to go," she announced, giving them two thumbs up.

The lights at the Strong home were turned off. Four figures walked out the back door, dressed in black, all carrying equipment bags. Duke followed them, tail wagging in large, slow sweeps and stood close to Greg. The dog somehow sensed the urgency of this moment. Greg locked the back door to the house and slid behind the wheel of the van. With a single motion of Greg's hand tapping his chest, Duke leaped into Greg's lap and then onto the floor of the truck. The trip to the Toccoa, Georgia, airport took just under two hours.

Greg drove the speed limit, careful not to attract the attention of the police, even though he knew most of the police officers from that area would be taking their two hour dinner break, asleep at home or hanging out at a girlfriend's house. He turned off the van's lights as he pulled up to the locked gate of the closed airport.

Pete jumped from the van and, holding a small flashlight in his mouth, pulled his lock picks from his pocket. Four years ago, he won first place in a lock picking contest sponsored by the D.E.A. office in Miami. Better than any thief, Pete was brilliant when it came to opening locks. Thirty seconds later, Pete pulled the chain from around the chain-link fence and swung the gates open. The van pulled onto the parking ramp and stopped.

Maggie stepped from the van and walked a short distance to the small airport building. She taped a small note to the office door which read, "Hi, Tom, it's Maggie. I got an emergency call to go home to Jersey. My dad is ill. See you in a few days. I hopped the fence. I knew you wouldn't mind. Please apologize to the neighbors."

Maggie's good friend, Tom, the airport's sole employee, respected and liked her. A quiet man, he wasn't prone to gossip and Maggie knew he wouldn't mention her flight to anyone.

Greg drove toward the Twin Beech that sat tied down at one corner of the airport. The plane was one of six made specifically for the CIA's involvement in the Vietnam war.

As the van approached the plane, Pete spoke. "Halderman arranged for our aircraft to be assigned to an operative named Mario and, of course, no last name. He also arranged for the Pentagon paperwork on the aircraft to be listed as out of service. As I always like to say, that plane is as clean as a rookie's locker."

Since Maggie's plane was also a Twin Beech, it would be easy for her to fly the aircraft without training. Her concern was she couldn't locate any of the registration documents but figured it mattered little under the circumstances. If they were intercepted, that would be the last thing on her mind.

According to Pete, the aircraft was used by a Miami corporation known as "The Company" and was utilized to move supplies during the war. In mint condition, the aircraft had the latest state of the art electronics. Extra fuel tanks took up part of the bay area. There was still plenty of room to suit the needs of the team.

Maggie jumped from the van and climbed into the aircraft to prepare for take-off while Greg backed the van to the aircraft's open side cargo door. The plane's door was designed to open on side tracks that ran inside the belly of the cargo bay. The door could be opened with ease while in flight to suit the needs of war-time maneuvers.

Greg swung the rear doors of the van open and, once again, the large sheet of reinforced plywood served as a ramp between the van and the aircraft. Using an electric cargo wench mounted inside the plane, the large slab rolled onto the aircraft with Greg and Bill guiding it. Equipment bags and a folded cage were stored by strapping them to the floor. Once the plane was loaded, Pete drove the van from the airport to a small service road just outside the airport.

Maggie turned in her seat to see if Greg, Bill and Duke were aboard. She called out, "Remember, once I start this first engine, we have about ten minutes to get the hell out of here. Are we ready?"

Receiving a thumbs-up from her team, she looked at Bill, remembering what he had said the day before. Once she started her engines there was no turning back. They smiled at one another and then she called out "clear" and the first of the huge Pratt and Whitney radial engines came to life, shattering the silence of the night.

Bill sat with a tiny flashlight in his mouth, reviewing his check list and counting equipment. Turning the light off, Bill called out, "We're good to go."

Again Maggie called out to her companions, "Clear," and cranked the final engine.

The small town of Toccoa had passed an ordinance requiring the airport to close at sundown. Homes had grown around the airfield and citizens were adamant about having peace and quiet at night.

The roar of the two engines was deafening. Greg settled into the co-pilot's seat and placed the headset over his ears. Greg and Maggie smiled at each other but said nothing. They had to move fast. Folks living in the neighborhood would be furious about the sound of the engines and, knowing the airport was closed, would call the police. Fortunately, they wouldn't respond quickly as they considered noise at the airport a low priority call.

With the cargo door still open, Maggie taxied the aircraft onto the runway. Duke stood in the belly, looking out the open bay area, excited to be moving.

With Greg's assistance, Maggie went over her final check list, checking the gauges, generators' output and fuel pressure. In the interim, Pete was jogging back to the airport gate. He was in the best physical condition he had been in since his divorce and wasn't even breathing hard by the time he reached the gate. Locking it behind him he ran toward the plane and hopped into the bay area, greeted by Duke who licked his face. Pete shut and locked the cargo door, motioning to Maggie to take off.

She revved the engines for takeoff. With lights off the Twin Beech roared down the runway. The roar from the two huge engines shook the neighborhood to life. She eased the control column forward, lifting the rear wheel from the runway. The aircraft gained speed as Greg pulled the small microphone closer to his mouth.

Greg spoke to Maggie, using his intercom mic, "We are V1; rotate."

With one hand on the throttles, Maggie pulled back on the control column, lifting the aircraft ten feet above the runway. The plane continued to gain speed, using the runway for lift. Maggie pulled back further on the control column and the plane bolted into the sky.

It was a beautiful, moon-lit night and visibility was perfect. Maggie banked the aircraft hard seventy degrees and caught a glimpse of a police car's flashing lights heading for the airport. She leveled the aircraft and flew south through the center of Georgia and, avoiding an area of storms near Jacksonville, decided to fly through the center of Florida as well.

Watchdog radar stations along the east coast of Florida wouldn't be alerted to an aircraft eighty miles west of the scan. She adjusted the navigation to an electronic VOR beacon on the tip of Pahokee, a small village south of Lake Okeechobee. The plane's autopilot navigated the aircraft south-southeast, following U.S. Highway 27 through the Everglades.

During flight, Bill and Pete unfolded the collapsed stainless steel monkey cage and assembled it into a three foot wire cubicle. They lifted the cage onto the cement block. Four inch stainless steel washers were placed over each of the four protruding bolts and secured with self locking nuts.

Bill scribbled on a blank sheet of paper, *Mayor Harkin's new waterfront property.*

"I knew this assignment would be exciting, but I never thought it would be this much fun," Bill laughed as he taped the sign to the cage.

Pete shook his head. "You're one sick dude, you know that?"

Bill hesitated, gathering his thoughts. "Me...sick? I never shot my informant because he had bad breath. Now that's sick."

"That was an accident and you know it," Pete replied with anger. "And since you brought that up, I never shot my dog because he ripped my back door screen. The damn dog saved your fucking kid from drowning and you killed it for ripping your screen, you low life piece of shit."

Riley laughed but was furious, "Yeah, Pete, your dog died after smelling your old lady's crotch."

Pete reached out, grabbed Bill's collar and cocked his arm to throw a punch. Greg leaned over his seat in the cockpit and shouted.

"Take it outside. We have a mission here. What the hell is wrong with you two?"

Pete released his grip.

"Leave my old lady out of this." Pete demanded. "Don't bring her up again. I mean it; you're on dangerous ground with this. Leave it alone."

Duke's ears perked up at hearing the command word "leave" and looked around the aircraft for a possible villain. Not finding a challenge, he lowered his head and went back to sleep.

"Ooooh, I'm scared big bad Pete's going to get me if I bring up his woman again," Riley joked.

Greg turned again in his seat and looked back at Bill.

"Ease up, Riley. We don't need this right now. Pete, I need you up here."

Pete leaned forward between the front seats of the aircraft and stared through the front windshield.

"See that glow out there?" Greg pointed. That's the Ft. Lauderdale skyline. I always love looking at that skyline."

"Will you ever move back to South Florida?" Pete asked.

"Nah, I'm done with Miami, police work and all that goes with it."

Maggie reached out and switched off the autopilot. Adjusting her position, she banked the aircraft to the east and headed toward a building standing alone at the edge of the Everglades.

National Electronics, Inc. was built by the Central Intelligence Agency in 1968. It supplied electronic surveillance equipment for a secret corporation known as "The Company" and other law enforcement agencies who could afford their expensive prices. The complex stood alone, far west of the city. Its companions were saw grass and palmetto shrubs. On the backside of the building, running from east to west, a wide roadway to nowhere was, in reality, an airstrip. A striped white line down the center and hidden strip lighting made it difficult to distinguish from any other roadway.

Pete had arranged with the president of NEI for them to land the plane on the tiny airstrip and have it refueled. The airstrip was built so the CIA could fly personnel to secret destinations.

Passing her last navigation point, Maggie dropped 2,000 feet and turned toward Ft. Lauderdale. Greg reached forward and changed the frequency of the radio to prepare to activate the runway's landing lights. The glow of city lights drew closer while, below, the spooky Everglades lay dark and eerie.

The plane dropped to 1,000 feet before Maggie keyed the radio's microphone three times, turning on the runway landing lights. Stunned at how close she was to the lit airstrip, she chopped the power, dropped the nose and set full flaps. Maggie brought the craft toward the airstrip, passing over the top of the factory's roof, missing it by ten feet. The aircraft touched down and Maggie killed the airstrip lighting and navigation lights. Coming to a dead stop, Maggie pivoted the aircraft and taxied back toward the building.

She shut down the engines next to two above ground fueling tanks sitting next to the building. The team knew the aircraft would be allowed to stay there for one day. Tomorrow morning, an NEI employee would fuel the aircraft.

Pete jumped from the open bay door and walked toward

a white panel truck with magnetic signs on each door which read, "D and J Plumbing, Miami, Florida," with a bogus phone number.

Everyone piled into the van for the forty five minute ride to Miami Beach. Later, the four team members checked into adjoining rooms at the Park Motel, 9th Street and Alton Rd. in Miami Beach. Once inside, Bill lit a match to the checklist, turning loose of it as it began to burn his fingers. The small piece of lit paper fell into the toilet bowl and was flushed.

"Sleep, we gotta sleep, it's already after seven in the morning. We must all be alert for this. No screw-ups," Greg announced as he fell to the bed. Within an hour, all four were sound asleep.

***

At 6 PM Pete drove the plumbing truck down Euclid Avenue.

"There it is, on your left, 1234 Euclid. She lives in Apartment 4. Park over there," Greg pointed, having spotted a legal spot that would suit their needs.

Pete backed the panel truck into the last parking spot in the area.

"Harkin will park a block or two away and walk to her apartment. That's what he always does. He'll be in there about thirty minutes, get laid and then head for his poker game," Greg spoke with confidence.

"How long has he been screwing this hooker bitch?" Pete asked.

"You won't believe this, but she's not a hooker. She's in love with the jerk. I know he gives her money, but she doesn't turn tricks. She's a bank teller at Financial Federal on Lincoln Road. She knows he's married but doesn't care. This thing has been going on for years. Even the guys he plays poker with don't know. She is closed mouth and so is he."

"Mayor Harkin, closed mouth, you gotta be kidding?" Bill laughed. "He never shuts up."

Greg raised his finger to make a point. "Here's my prediction, Billy boy. Once the mayor turns up missing, she won't say a word to anyone and will pine away. She'll never hand him up. And as far as our illustrious mayor is concerned, he won't have much to say after this night. That's why this plan is so beautiful."

"Good point, Greg, good point," Bill conceded.

Greg grabbed Bill's shoulder to turn him slightly and then pointed out the front windshield. "Here he comes, right on schedule, wearing that stupid fisherman's hat. What an asshole!"

Mayor Harkin walked down the dimly lit street, slump shouldered with his hands in his pockets. He was wearing a light grey silk Nik Nik shirt with a large picture of a penguin sporting a white scarf, a top hat and cane on the back of the shirt. He turned into the apartment complex and entered Apartment 4 without knocking.

Greg reached into his equipment bag and removed the small, compact, CO_2 rifle. He opened a small plastic container, revealing four small darts. Removing one of the darts, Greg opened the chamber of the rifle and slid the dart into place. Closing the chamber and locking it, he charged his weapon with CO_2.

"I'm ready. Pull the side panel open a little and let's see what I can do from this point," Greg ordered.

Bill pulled the side panel door open and Greg raised his rifle to his shoulder. Looking down the barrel, he noticed his stub where his ring finger used to be. As he looked into the rifle's scope, he became angry and felt justified at what he was about to do. His heart was beating faster now, in anticipation of the moment to come.

"Perfect. My position is perfect. When Harkin turns onto the sidewalk to head for his car, I'll have a perfect shot. Let's do it. We're good to go."

Maggie reached over and attached the leash to Duke's collar. Jumping from the truck, Duke dashed to a nearby grassy area to relieve himself, dragging Maggie behind him.

Bill removed the 9 mm semiautomatic from an equipment bag and shoved it into his waistband, covering it with his black shirt. He shoved a ski mask into a cargo pocket in his pants. Putting on a light windbreaker, he stepped from the van and adjusted his weapon to make it more comfortable, hoping he wouldn't have to use it.

As Maggie walked Duke toward the apartment, Bill crossed the street and sat in a lawn chair on the front porch of the next apartment building. He knew if he remained quiet and still, he wouldn't be seen as the street lights on Euclid Ave. offered poor lighting to the area. Most of the apartment entrances ran perpendicular to the street and had no lighting.

Greg and Pete sat in the truck, waiting for one of the

most prominent persons in Miami Beach to finish what was to become his last orgasm.

Greg reached forward to touch Pete's shoulder. "I owe you big time for this one, Pete. You're a good friend, risking yourself for this. Did I ever thank you?"

Pete turned in his driver's seat to face Greg, "About a hundred times. You would do the same for me."

Greg nodded in agreement and the two sat, staring at the entrance to the apartment.

"How long did you tell me he's been humping this broad?" Pete asked.

"Over three years I know of," Greg responded. "Her name is Gloria Rankin...not that pretty, but Harkin thinks so. She loves the creep and would do nothing to hurt him. She also knows he'll never divorce his old lady but she doesn't care."

Pete smiled and reached for his money clip. "I've got twenty bucks in my pocket that says when he turns up missing she'll go to the police and tell all. What da ya say, old man?" Pete asked.

"You're on, sucker. And it won't be love that keeps her closed mouth, it'll be fear. If she gives up her lover, she'll have to quit her job and leave town. She has family here. No, she'll say nothing to no one and I'll be twenty bucks richer," Greg laughed. "And how would you like to lose another twenty? I'll bet you the poker guys don't call his house when he's a no-show."

Pete put his money back in his pocket. "Nah, I won't take that bet. Every guy in that game has a little something on the side and because of that they won't call his house."

FRED WOOLDRIDGE

A marked uniformed police car slowly turned off 12th Street onto Euclid Avenue and headed north right toward them. Bill spotted it first and walked from his porch seat to a darkened position between two buildings. Plastering himself flat against the wall, he disappeared from sight.

"Oh, shit," Pete said, "It's a damn squad car."

Pete slid down from his driver's position, placing his knees on the floor of the truck, careful not to touch the brake pedal.

Greg was invisible, sitting in the back of the van, and froze as the marked police car rolled by.

"If he saw anything he didn't like, he'll make another pass. How are we doing on time?" Greg whispered.

Pete reached down and pressed the small button on his watch, illuminating it. "He's due out in another ten minutes or so. Why do I have this feeling this whole thing is about to turn to shit?"

Greg chuckled under his breath and responded. "I've spent my whole adult life living like this. We're going to do this thing tonight, damn it."

The patrol car turned onto 14th Street, headed west and disappeared. Riley walked from his hiding place and returned to his seat on the nearby porch. Minutes passed. Nothing happened. Maggie continued to walk Duke back and forth in front of the apartment. Everyone waited. Thirty minutes came and went and still no mayor. Pete was getting anxious and nervous, but Greg sat motionless, his rifle cradled in his arms. It was obvious to Pete that Greg was in his "Predator" mentality. He had seen Greg like this many times over the years.

"Is he going for seconds, or what?" Pete joked.

"Soon, my friend; be patient," Greg answered, without taking his eyes off the entrance to Gloria's apartment.

Several more minutes passed. Then the door to Apartment 4 opened. It was dark inside the apartment and Greg strained to see his target. There was no movement and then a head looked out. Someone walked out of the apartment and toward the sidewalk. Greg could tell it was the mayor by his gait.

"Here he comes, let's do it," Greg whispered.

Pete started his engine, a signal to Bill and Maggie the moment had come. Maggie and Duke were positioned ten feet from where the mayor would approach the sidewalk. Bill sat, looking in the opposite direction from the mayor's position. Greg slid the side panel door open about four inches and pulled his rifle to his shoulder. His heart was racing, but he felt in complete command of his emotions. He had felt like this many times over the years and was always able to maintain control.

Greg couldn't believe what he was seeing. The same uniformed police car turned south onto Euclid and started to make another pass by the apartment building.

"What the hell brought him back, damn it?" Pete asked, as he slid back down in his seat, turning off the engine.

Greg shut the door of the panel truck and whispered, "It's Maggie. He's taking a second look at Maggie. Good looking blond and a big German shepherd is always worthy of a second look."

The team watched the mayor reach the sidewalk. When Harkin spotted the police car approaching, he turned and walked back to the apartment. He tried the door but it was locked. He knocked but no one came.

The squad car rolled to a stop right in front of where Maggie and Duke were standing.

Greg whispered to Pete, "Let's hope he's a rookie and doesn't know her."

The officer's window rolled down, revealing a face Maggie didn't recognize.

The officer smiled at her and spoke, "Beautiful dog you have there. What's his name?"

Wanting to let the officer know she was married, she responded. "His name is Rocky. My husband always wanted to call his dog Rocky. Is there a problem in the area, officer? I noticed you before when you drove by."

"Oh, no, M'am, it's just my normal routine patrol pattern. You have a good evening."

The officer, discouraged over hearing Maggie was married, rolled up his window and continued north.

The mayor stood frozen next to the entrance of Gloria's apartment until he saw the patrol car was gone.

"Start the truck, Pete, here he comes," Greg whispered.

The mayor reached the sidewalk and, after looking both ways, pulled his cap down above his eyes and proceeded south toward his car. Bill walked onto the sidewalk toward Mayor Harkin. Greg slid the side panel door open and raised his weapon. The rifle scope self-focused on the back of the mayor's shirt. Greg aimed, placing the cross hairs on the shirt's penguin head. He squeezed the trigger. The weapon made a soft pop sound as the dart exited the barrel at 800 feet a second, striking its target. The barbed needle entered

Harkin's body right between his shoulder blades and injected the mixture of Sodium Pentothal and Ace Promazine close to his spinal cord. The drugs would have an immediate effect on Harkin.

Harkin seemed stunned at first and then panicked as he tried to reach for the dart. Unable to do so, he started to return to Gloria's apartment and bumped into Bill Riley.

"Good evening, Mr. Mayor, how ya doing?"

Pete pulled the truck from its parking spot and drove the short distance to where Harkin was standing.

"You must have me confused with someone else," the mayor uttered, his speech becoming slurred.

Greg slid the truck's side door wide open. Maggie walked over to assist Riley and the two steered the dizzy politician toward the street. He stumbled as he stepped from the sidewalk and had to be held. Greg reached out and pulled him into the truck and Maggie, Duke and Riley followed. The door slid shut and the truck drove away. The capture was over in thirty seconds.

"If there was a witness to this, they wouldn't know what they saw," Pete chuckled.

"Excuse me, but I have to get to my card game," the mayor whispered with a thick tongue. Drool ran from the corner of his mouth as he grinned at seeing Captain Strong for the first time.

"Is that you, Captain? How are you? And how is Maggie?"

"Just fine, Mr. Mayor, she's sitting right next to you. Why don't you try to get some sleep?"

Harkin stared at Maggie for a long time, trying to focus and then raised a hand to wave at her. He closed his eyes.

Greg reached out to pull the politician forward in his seat, revealing the dart stuck in his back. Unscrewing the dart from its needle, Greg placed it back in its container. He removed a large self-adhesive gauze pad from the equipment bag and slipped it under the mayor's shirt to cover the protruding needle. A small spot of blood appeared on the mayor's shirt. "There, that should keep you from oozing blood all over my truck."

Harkin woke from his stupor, "Are we going to my card game? They're expecting me. I shouldn't be late," the mayor smiled.

"Yes, we are. But you must rest," Greg responded.

Pete turned onto the Julia Tuttle causeway and headed for the NEI building. Mayor Harkin's eyes drooped and saliva continued to run from the corner of his mouth as he sat in semi-consciousness. Fearful saliva would be left in the truck, Greg taped a gauze pad under his victim's chin.

Forty minutes later the white panel truck pulled onto Pembroke Rd. and headed west to their waiting plane.

"I always liked you, Captain," the mayor spoke, surprising Greg he was awake.

"Yeah, right! That's why you ordered me killed," Greg snapped back.

Harkin lowered his head and reached out to touch Greg but couldn't raise his arm. "I'm very sorry about that. I had no choice."

"You son-of-a-bitch! Did you hear that, Maggie, he had no choice? Your kid knocked up your housekeeper and when she blackmailed you, you had her killed. Then you bribed the Medical Examiner to call it a suicide."

Harkin's eyes grew heavy as he drifted back to sleep but Greg kept talking. "You have the balls to say you had no choice? With blood tests, I could have proven that baby belonged to your low-life son, but I couldn't keep the M.E from cremating the housekeeper's body. I went to the Grand Jury with what I had but they wouldn't give me a warrant because you interfered. Then you hired some punk from Toronto to have me killed. Now it's my turn."

Riley knew Greg had grown emotional and reached out to squeeze his arm. "Save your breath. This bastard's not hearing a word of it. Now we're in control and, you're right, it's your turn."

Maggie sat stunned. Up to this point she wasn't convinced Harkin had ordered Greg's assassination. She only had Pete's word and wasn't sure if he was lying. She wanted to strike out at Harkin but resisted the urge. She sat, teeming with anger.

Finally, the panel truck pulled into the NEI complex and turned onto the runway, parking next to the Twin Beech. Pushing the panel door open, Maggie hopped from the van, stopping to take deep breaths before walking to the plane. Pete reached forward to unlock and open the cargo doors of the aircraft.

Greg and Bill lifted Harkin from the truck and placed him in the plane's cargo bay. No longer able to speak or move his limbs, Harkin fought to stay awake.

"Pete, give us a hand with this fat bastard," Bill called out.

The three team members struggled to get Harkin into the steel monkey cage. Then the door was shut and locked.

"We have a situation here, Greg," Maggie said, placing both hands high above her head to feel the wind blowing steady out of the west.

"The damn wind never blows this hard out of the west this time of the year. This'll be a problem for us."

Greg stood next to Maggie and could feel the strong, steady breeze blowing out of the Everglades.

"I'm guessing ten knots. You'll have to take off into the wind. We have no choice," Greg said as he held one hand over his head to feel the wind's direction.

Maggie looked down, hesitating before she spoke. "Not good, baby. If we do that, we chance not clearing the building and the tower behind it. With the auxiliary tanks full and one extra person on board we're too heavy. We have one shot at this and have no good choices."

Again, Maggie hesitated before speaking further. She wanted to make sure she was making accurate decisions and had considered everything possible. She grabbed Greg by the arm and walked with him to the nose of the plane before speaking.

"This should be our decision, not the team's We can abandon the plan; you take care of the mayor in the Everglades and then apologize to NEI officials for not getting the plane off their runway. Or we can risk taking off down wind and killing ourselves when we run out of runway. For certain, by taking off into the wind, I'm going to slam into that building!"

When Greg spoke, it was obvious he was angry. "I'm not dumping the plan, Maggie. We've gone too far to back off. And I can't allow this to become a murder investigation.

There can be no body. I say let's take our chances and take off with the wind. What da ya think, can you do it? You're the best pilot I've ever known."

Maggie laughed, "Your prejudice is showing." She stared into the dark field east of the runway. The moon provided enough light to see there were no trees or large obstructions in their way.

Again, Maggie hesitated before speaking. She was frightened she would let the team down. "Maybe, just maybe, if I can get wheels up before the pavement ends, it'll work. But the wheels should be off the ground because the sand is soft and mushy. If we run into the sand before we get some lift, we'll sink. There's nothing but sawgrass and scrub palm in front of us. This damn plane is like a truck and we'll just mow it down. Maybe...just maybe we'll make it. I'm praying for feather-light weight if the wheels do roll onto the sand. Like I said, we have no good choices."

Riley called from the bay door of the aircraft. "We gotta get out of here. Whadaya say? Harkin is getting more alert. If he starts screaming, I'll shoot the bastard."

Everyone huddled together as Maggie studied the situation. It was all in her hands and she knew it.

Greg broke the silence. "Why the hell did the CIA build a runway right up to the edge of the building?"

Pete had an immediate response. "See those big sliding doors. They keep a special built coal black one seat mini jet loaded with surveillance equipment inside. When they go for a mission, the pilot lights up inside the building, then the doors are slid open and the takeoff starts from there. They land the same way."

Accepting Pete's answer, Maggie looked toward Greg for support. He stood facing her, without expression, looking into her eyes.

"It's your call, Maggie, whatever you say, we back you, but Harkin will go down tonight, one way or the other," Greg assured her.

"You're right, baby, it's my call and I've just made it," Maggie said with confidence. "First, we're dumping everything we don't need. Greg, get the tool box and life raft from the back side compartment and leave it against the building. I want Pete and Bill to go though the front side bins and empty everything, including the tire repair kit and air pump. If they're not sure of something, ask me. Also, move Harkin's cage aft a few feet so I can generate a little more lift from the wings."

While the team hurried to empty the aircraft of weight, Maggie removed the chocks from the aircraft's wheels.

"Everyone out of the aircraft and back away while I move the plane up close to the building," Maggie shouted. She started the engines and taxied the aircraft toward the building. As she approached, she pivoted the craft, causing the right wing to barely miss the building as it spun around. As she continued to swing the aircraft around, the tail lined up close to the building. The tail was now inches from the wall.

"Let's get the hell out of here. We're losing precious time," Maggie called out.

Everyone hopped into the plane through the bay door. Duke barked with excitement. Greg slammed the bay door shut while Maggie increased her rpm's, blowing dust, old grass clippings and a McDonald's container into the air. Greg climbed into the right seat and placed the headphones around his neck. He began instrument checks, wondering what they would do if they experienced a problem with the engines or hydraulics.

Maggie leaned back, turning her head, and called to Riley and Spoto. "You better tie your asses to something, this might get bumpy. And leash Duke to a cargo tie-down."

Riley laughed, "I've already tied myself to Pete 'cause he's never going to die. Luckiest son-of-a-bitch I ever met."

Mayor Harkin peered through his cage at the two men strapping themselves down to the aircraft. Still speaking with a slur, he said, "Could I have a drink of water?"

He couldn't be heard over the roar of the engines. Harkin had pulled the bandage from his chin, indicating the effects of the drugs were wearing off. Realizing he couldn't be heard, he spoke louder. "Excuse me, I need water. May I speak to Captain Strong? I need to get to my poker game. Why am I here? What's going on?"

"Shut up, you asshole," Riley shouted over the roar of the engines. Then he banged on the cage and looked toward Duke. "Get 'em, Duke!"

Duke lunged at Harkin, barking and snapping. Hearing Duke, Greg turned in his seat and yelled. "What the hell are you doing, Riley? Duke, leave it. Leave it now. Leash the damn dog to a cargo tie, Riley."

Greg pulled the headset to his ears. "Are you ready, baby?"

"Hell, no, I'm not ready. I should be home in my kitchen, whipping up a batch of mountain pudding," Maggie joked.

Maggie saw the look on Greg's face and smiled. "I'm kidding, I'm just scared. I'm ready. Let's do it."

She watched Greg reach over and place his left hand over her right, clutching tightly to the throttle controls between the two seats. Placing both feet on the brakes, she shoved hard on both pedals, locking down the brakes. Maggie shoved the throttles forward and the huge Pratt and Whitney engines roared to life. Hurricane force winds blasted the building wall and surrounding area. Maggie watched a plastic spoon whirl past the windshield making circles in the air, plastering itself to the wall of the building.

The aircraft shuttered, vibrating violently. "I feel like I'm on a bull waiting to be released from its pen," Maggie shouted into the microphone. She lifted both her feet from the brakes and the aircraft lunged forward. Maggie held her breath. As the aircraft rolled down the runway, it gained speed slowly, then faster and faster. Maggie fixed her eyes on the dark field ahead.

"I don't know, Maggie, we're not even sixty knots and we're running out of runway," Greg spoke into his microphone.

"Don't talk," Maggie snapped back. "We're committed."

The aircraft ran off the end of the runway, across a short gravel area and onto the soft, sandy field.

"Shit, shit, shit," Maggie shouted as the aircraft began to bounce and tip.

She could feel the plane was light on its wheels. It shook violently as it crossed the field of sand, mowing down palmetto scrubs and sawgrass. The stall warning lights flashed and the alarm seemed deafening.

The aircraft had gained enough speed that the wheels

didn't sink into the sand but not enough for a full lift. The rear wheel was up in normal position as the front wheels tore through the sawgrass and small scrubs. Maggie knew she couldn't allow the plane to settle back into the sand. She finessed the control column like a talented musician plays an instrument. Then, she saw it. Far out in the darkness stood a sixty foot Florida pine tree in their path.

"Shit, shit, shit, we're not going to make it!" Maggie screamed over the roar of the engines.

The front wheels lifted from the field and she held the aircraft steady at five feet above the ground. The tree was coming up fast.

"Good job, Maggie, we're airborne," Greg complimented her.

"Not yet. See that tree in front of us? We need to stay low, using ground effect to get more speed."

The aircraft climbed to seven feet and Maggie held elevation as the plane continued to gain speed and the tree grew closer. Then slowly, she pulled back on the control column and the aircraft began to climb. Maggie banked the aircraft to the right. The left wing tore through the outer branches of the huge tree, clipping off leaves and branch stems.

"Yes, yes," Maggie shouted.

Greg was already smiling when she looked toward him. "I love you, baby. Gimme five," Greg said as he held out his hand for a slap.

"Ah, but only when I save your ass," she kidded.

Greg looked back at the blank expressions on the faces of his two companions. They never realized the danger or the skill it took to pull off this near perfect take-off.

Mayor Harkin sat in his cage, eyes closed with his head slumped forward.

"Good, let Harkin sleep it off. I want him alert. I've got to sleep myself. I'm exhausted," Greg apologized.

Maggie flew southwest out over the Gulf of Mexico, then banked south, setting the navigation for the western tip of Cuba. Once there, she would bank the aircraft back to the east and head for the Grand Cayman Islands, 430 miles away on the edge of the Caribbean Sea. Her destination was the famous Cayman Trench, between Jamaica and the Cayman Islands.

The trench, almost five miles deep at one spot, would be the perfect place for Mayor Harkin's new home. Even submarines couldn't locate such a small object at that depth and if they could, little would be done about it.

The mayor would be eaten by small fish and thousands of tiny limpets, small shell-like creatures that thrive on anything dead that falls into the trench. In less than two weeks, there would be nothing left of him but a skeleton.

Once excitement of the take-off was over, Greg, exhausted, drifted off to sleep. Looking at him reminded Maggie that her husband was still not the person he was prior to the shooting. She reached over and lifted the earphones from his head. Later, she would help him insert an IV into his arm. Since eating food might make him sick, Greg planned on staying nourished with the IV until he got home the next day.

Everyone but Maggie dozed off. She leaned back in her seat, staring into the black sky in front of her. The auto pilot moved the control column, making corrections.

Now a kidnapper and soon to be a murderer, Maggie

pondered why she wasn't more nervous or upset with herself. She found the adventure exciting as she retraced the events of the abduction, her encounter with the police officer and the scary take-off that had made her adrenaline pump fast. She rationalized she wasn't killing Harkin but was just an accessory to murder.

Both Riley and Spoto had volunteered to shove the cage out the bay door but Greg insisted the pleasure would be his.

An hour later, the aircraft hit an air pocket, jolting Maggie from her doze. She sat erect in her seat. She realized she had nodded off, a symptom of adrenaline draining from her bloodstream. Her eyes stared into the black sky as adrenaline recharged her body. Seeing nothing but darkness, she scanned the instrument panel for problems. Whispering to herself, she went through her checklist, "Fuel good, generators check, altitude good, autopilot on, course setting on target...well, almost." Confident all was good, she tried to settle herself.

She lifted her thermos to her lips and gulped the lukewarm coffee without using the cup. With her heart still pumping, she took deep breaths to calm herself. She knew the aircraft had a poor navigation system so she re-checked the VOR and made a slight manual correction.

Maggie noticed everyone had slept through the scare except Mayor Harkin. He sat in his cage, staring at the red and green ready lights that control the cargo door. Now awake and no longer under the full influence of drugs, he realized this was more than a kidnapping. Dehydrated from the effects of the drugs, Harkin looked toward the cockpit and asked Maggie for a drink of water. Getting no response from Maggie, Harkin shouted, "I need a drink of water, damn it," and began banging on his cage with his hands.

Everyone woke. Greg leaned forward and scanned the instrument panel, noting their position.

"What time is it, Maggie?" Greg asked.

"Quarter to one. I want to start an IV for you," she answered.

"Nah, I'll do it, you fly." He slid from his seat and crawled to the rear of the aircraft to retrieve his overnight bag.

"Captain, we have to talk," the mayor demanded.

"Shut up or I'll tape your mouth shut," Greg ordered as he inserted the IV into his forearm with the skill of a nurse.

"You see this, you son-of-a-bitch? This is how I eat now because of you. I'm missing twelve feet of intestine, part of my lung and a finger. You were having me killed because your damn housekeeper got knocked up. You had that girl murdered. You're the ultimate scumbag."

Harkin clung to the cage with both hands and placed his face against the heavy wire grid. "You gave me no choice. She was costing me so much money. But you wouldn't let it go. So many people came to you on my behalf but you wouldn't let it go. It was your fault I went to such extremes."

Greg laughed, "Hey, everyone, did you hear that? It's my fault. He's blaming me for all of this."

"There's money. Lots of money if we can make this go away," Harkin pleaded. "Twenty thousand as soon as we land and another fifty in a week. I promise I'll say nothing about this."

"Yeah, right, and we all know how good your word is.

Besides, that's chicken-shit money. I don't want your money, I want your life," Greg shouted at him.

Another hour passed and nothing more was said about the money or the mayor's impending death. The aircraft began to smell of human waste. It had become obvious the illustrious political leader had a bowel movement in his pants while under the influence of the drugs, a common mishap.

Minutes crept by. To pass the time, Pete and Bill exchanged stories about informants they once shared. Greg had finished his IV feeding and returned to the co-pilot's seat. He found Maggie readjusting several controls.

"The autopilot on this plane is horrible," Maggie complained. "This is the third correction I've made since we took off. You would think the CIA could build a better system. Anyway, about ten more minutes, baby, and we'll be at the trench. Another five and you can dump your cargo. I need this to be over, how 'bout you?"

"Nah, Maggie, I'm savoring every minute," Greg smiled, leaning sideways to kiss his wife on the cheek. He scanned the instrument panel and noticed Maggie had repositioned the aircraft. For the first time, he could see a full moon. After a moment, Greg unbuckled himself and again climbed from his seat.

Before approaching Harkin's cage, he whispered to Maggie through his microphone, "Showtime," causing her to look around and smile.

Mayor Harkin was sensing the urgency of the moment and pleaded for his life. Greg unlocked three of the wheels to the cage, grabbing it from the top to stabilize it. Harkin reached up to touch Strong's fingers wrapped around the wire.

"Please, Greg, please, please don't do this. I'll do whatever you ask. Just please don't do this. Please, please, I beg you." Tears ran down the mayor's cheeks.

Greg pulled his hands from the cage. "Don't touch me, you piece of shit," he ordered.

"I won't touch you anymore...I won't, just don't do this, please. God, make him stop. Please, Greg, don't do this," Harkin was crying, a pathetic human.

Greg thought, *I wish his dead housekeeper could see him now, covered with his own human waste, slobbering like a baby, pleading for his life.*

"Two minutes," Maggie called out. She shoved the control column forward, setting the flaps at thirty degrees. The nose of the aircraft dropped until her altitude was about fifty feet above the ocean surface. Maggie leveled off and switched on the landing lights to better judge her altitude above the water.

Greg nodded to Pete and Bill and the three began to anchor themselves to the cargo ties on the floor of the plane while Harkin continued to plead for his life. Duke, harnessed to a cargo tie, sensed the urgency and began barking.

"Knock it off, Duke. Lie down!" Greg ordered.

Duke, as always, obeyed.

Riley reached forward to release the lock on the cargo door. The ready light turned bright red, indicating the door was ready for opening in flight.

"One minute," Maggie called out.

Greg nodded to Riley and the bay door of the plane was opened. High winds blew through the bay area and the roar of the Pratt and Whitney engines was deafening.

Startled, Duke jumped to his feet again and started barking but the wind and engines drowned out his bark. It was now impossible to communicate without use of the intercom.

The mayor's hair blew about his head. He grabbed the cage, pressing his face to the front wire, screaming "No, no, no," but his voice was drowned out by the roar of the wind and engines.

"Now," Maggie called to Greg through the intercom. "Now, baby. You have a one minute window to get this done."

Greg reached forward, unlocking the remaining wheel to the death chamber.

"Hey, Harkin," Greg shouted, "You want a drink of water? Well, here's your fuckin' drink of water."

With his back against the wall of the aircraft, Greg placed both feet on the cage and pushed hard, causing the cage to lunge toward the dark sky. It disappeared from the aircraft.

The force of the one hundred mile per hour winds outside the aircraft caused the mayor's head to slam against the cage, fracturing his skull and rendering him unconscious. The cage fell, hitting the water in seconds. Greg knew that Mayor Harkin would be dead in less than a minute. He envisioned his body drifting to the top of the cage as it continued to descend to the cold ocean floor. Greg calculated it would take about an hour for Harkin to reach his new home, over seven miles below the surface.

Riley reached forward and slammed the bay door closed, shutting out the wind and noise. The three men sat in silence, staring at one another. After a moment, Riley broke the silence.

"Hey, the guy needed a drink of water, what the hell."

Greg looked at Riley with disgust, "Shut up, Riley. Don't be funny. I just killed a man."

CHAPTER EIGHT

Maggie lifted the nose of the aircraft to two hundred feet altitude and leveled off while her three companions untied themselves from the cargo floor. No one spoke or smiled, and there were no high fives or handshakes. Greg crawled to the front of the aircraft and slid into the right seat before speaking to Maggie. "Let's get outta here."

She banked the aircraft, careful to watch the altitude. Then she set navigation to a VOR just on the western tip of Cuba. Engaging the autopilot, Maggie watched the instruments as the aircraft corrected to her settings. Without looking at her husband, she spoke.

"Now comes the hard part. I've got to watch the altimeter. At two hundred feet elevation, we could be in the drink in a split second. As long as our weather holds, we're good, but if it worsens, we'll have to gain altitude. The higher our altitude, the bigger chance we'll be detected on somebody's radar."

Greg nodded in agreement, staring out at the night sky. He waited a moment before changing the subject, then spoke into his microphone. "Pete was right about Harkin. In the last moment of his life, he admitted he hired the Canadian to kill me. You know what, Maggie? If I hadn't been gunned down, I would've eventually nailed his son for conspiracy to murder his housekeeper. The kid is still free and I'm flying across the Caribbean killing his father. Go figure. I'm relieved Harkin confessed. It made pushing him out that bay door easier for me. I could've done it anyway, but now I'm feeling less guilty."

Maggie smiled and reached out her hand to show her approval. The two sat holding hands as they raced home to plan their next mission.

"You sleep and I'll fly the first watch," Maggie volunteered.

"You gotta be kidding. I couldn't sleep after that experience," Greg laughed.

"Oh, bull, you could sleep on a roller coaster with the sun in your eyes," Maggie joked. "Who're you trying to kid? This is your wife you're talking to."

Greg smiled and closed his eyes. "I'll give it a try."

Maggie was right. Within ten minutes, her husband's breathing slowed. He was drifting off to sleep. Maggie looked back into the cargo bay. Pete and Bill had switched on a cargo light and were playing gin rummy. She turned back in her seat and stared out at the night. The weather was perfect. A full moon continued to light the sky and glisten off the calm ocean below. The wind was calm and the aircraft stable as it headed toward home. The altimeter stayed constant at two hundred feet elevation and Maggie made note that all the instruments were within acceptable range. Except for the cop circling back and the scary takeoff, all had gone as planned.

Maggie spent the next hour thinking about how she had gotten to this night. The shooting of her husband, Pete's fake funeral and his visit with Nixon, coupled with Riley's firing from the police department, had brought them all together to form a team of murderers. She still couldn't bring herself to trust Pete, but since Greg did, she had convinced herself that her feelings were based on all the prior baggage he had brought into their marriage.

She recalled her discussion with the team about its next assignment. Pedro Macedo was the biggest and most ruthless cocaine trafficker in all of Colombia. He would be a lot more difficult to kill than Mayor Harkin, except they wouldn't have to hide the body. Macedo was well protected and killing a drug cartel figure deep in his own Colombian backyard would require much planning. She still wondered why Pete had been so insistent they make no plans or decisions on Macedo until Harkin was dead. "One mission at a time," he would say.

Moments later, Maggie thought she spotted something off her left wing. She stared into the dark sky for over a minute. Seeing nothing, she forgot about what might have been there. Ten minutes later, she glanced out the left window again just to double-check. Her heart jumped and she sat upright in her seat. She punched her husband who woke. Greg looked at her to see why he was awakened. Maggie leaned back in her seat so Greg could see past her and have a better look out the window.

"Oh, shit! How long has that been there?" Greg asked.

Maggie shook her head. "I don't know. I thought I saw something before, but then it disappeared. Got any ideas?"

Two hundred feet off their left wing was a coal black F4 Phantom jet fighter with no identifiable markings.

Greg leaned over his seat and shouted to Pete and Bill, "Hey, check this out."

The team stared at the jet fighter, hoping their eyes were deceiving them.

"From its looks, I'm guessing it's CIA. I know for sure there's one just like that in a hangar at Miami International," Pete said without taking his eyes off the mystery aircraft.

"Oh yeah, well, what the hell's it doing way out here?" Bill asked.

Greg interrupted, "Where are we, Maggie?"

"Ah...we're southeast of the Isle of Youth, south of the Cuban mainland, heading northwest. We'll be passing close to the western tip of Cuba in less than a half hour," Maggie responded.

Greg pulled a navigation chart from a door pocket and held it up for Pete and Bill to see. "Pete, I'm guessing you're wrong about it belonging to the CIA. I think it belongs to Castro. Look at our current position and how close we are to Cuba. If they own that sucker, we're in deep shit if they think we're going to cross their country at this altitude. They may shoot us down. If we gain altitude, we chance being detected by American radar. Anyone have any ideas?"

"I disagree, Greg," Maggie chimed in. "Cuba doesn't own radar sophisticated enough to spot aircraft below two hundred feet, and they don't fly F4 Phantom's; they fly Russian MiGs. Unless that pilot just stumbled upon us, I'm guessing this fighter jet is not from Cuba and this is a lot more sinister than an air space violation. In any case, it's not good. I suggest we change course, head west southwest and away from Cuba. Let's see what happens."

Everyone agreed.

Maggie switched off the autopilot and banked the aircraft to the west, nudging it closer to the F4. *The bastard is in my way. He's crowding me toward the mainland and I ain't goin'*, Maggie thought as she got closer and closer to the fighter. When they were less than fifty feet apart, Maggie slowed the aircraft so the fighter couldn't stay with her. The fighter lowered its nose and accelerated, disappearing into the night sky. The jet's backwash rocked the plane and Maggie struggled to regain control.

Once the aircraft stabilized, she looked at Greg. "Okay, that's good news. It's gone. I'll continue a more westward heading and away from the mainland. This might all be over."

"That was a gutsy move, Maggie. He could have thought you were being aggressive," Greg said.

"Yeah, right, I can see the headlines in the papers, Twin Beech attacks F4 Phantom," Maggie joked.

No sooner had Maggie spoken when the fighter reappeared in front and above them. The pilot rocked his wings and veered off again disappearing into the night sky. Maggie held her position. Less than a minute later, the jet returned again, but this time dropped to a position directly in front of plane. The jet wash from the fighter jet created severe, constant turbulence and Maggie struggled to maintain control of the plane. Once again, the fighter rocked its wings and veered off in another direction.

"Okay, this guy wants us to follow him, maybe to Havana. Greg, you might be right on this one. Since he can shoot us out of the sky at any time, I'm inclined to change heading and follow; any arguments?" Maggie asked.

Greg shook his head, "I'm not ready to give in to a pilot flying an unidentified aircraft that may or may not be Cuban. Like you said, Maggie, they don't own F4's. This is weird."

Greg reached for the microphone and changed the radio frequency to 121.5. Pulling the microphone close to his mouth, he spoke, "Beech 421A to unidentified aircraft, do you copy? Over."

There was silence as the team waited in anticipation of a response. Greg repeated his broadcast but added, "If you copy, flash your navigation lights. I repeat, flash your navigation lights."

The team sat bewildered. The mystery fighter jet didn't respond.

Without asking her husband, Maggie banked the aircraft east toward Cuba. The fighter jet reappeared and disappeared, making wide circles to maintain proximity. The fighter pulled in front of them, rocked his wings again and banked to the east. Maggie followed.

"I'm confused," Maggie said as she double-checked her navigation and heading. "If we maintain this heading, we'll skirt the southern coast of Cuba and pass within a short distance of Guantanamo Air Base."

"I told you the damn thing was CIA. Cuba owns Russian MiGs, not F4's," Pete said confidently.

Maggie laughed, "I don't see it makes much difference since we've been caught flying at two hundred feet elevation over restricted air space. Who cares who owns the damn aircraft?"

"You're wrong, Maggie, we're much better off with the CIA. We....I can talk our way out of this. You watch," Pete said.

When the two aircraft were about fifty miles from the airfield at Guantanamo, the jet rocked its wings and headed north over mainland Cuba.

"So much for your CIA theory, Pete," Maggie grumbled.

Once the two aircraft were inland five miles, the jet banked east and began to drop altitude. Maggie followed, staying far enough behind the mystery plane to keep jet wash at a minimum.

Up ahead, right in the middle of the Cuban jungle, was a small unlit airstrip. If it hadn't been for the full moon, she wouldn't have seen it. There were no buildings, vehicles or visible signs of life on or near the strip. The two aircraft continued to descend.

Maggie sized up the airstrip. "He'll never put that fighter down on that runway. Hell, I don't think I can land in that short a distance," she told Greg.

As the two aircraft continued to descend, the fighter lowered his landing gear, than pulled its nose up and disappeared above them.

"He wants us to land," Maggie said. "I think we should get weapons out. Everyone agree?"

Maggie made a pass alongside the airstrip to size it up.

"It's going to be tight. I want everyone to know if I'm lucky enough to land without killing all of us, we'll never be able to take off. Since we have no choices, everyone tie themselves down back there and shorten Duke's leash so he can't stand. I'm going in."

Maggie, banking the aircraft hard, checked for wind speed and direction by watching for movement in the tops of the jungle growth. It made little difference as the wind was non-existent. Once lined up with the airstrip, Maggie switched on the landing lights, throttled back, pushed the nose down and set her flaps to full. She continued to descend. She dropped the wheels, increased throttle and raised the nose. The aircraft shuttered and the stall warning horn sounded as she descended. Maggie lowered the nose to silence the alarm by increasing speed but it wouldn't shut off.

Riley shouted from the cargo bay, "I don't like this."

The instant Maggie was sure there was airstrip below her, she killed both engines and pushed the nose down. At three feet above the airstrip, the plane lost lift and slammed to the runway at seventy five mph. Maggie touched the floor pedals, engaging the brakes. She knew if she pushed too hard, the aircraft would flip, possibly killing everyone. She continued to work the brakes as she watched the jungle in front of her approach. When the aircraft was near the end of the runway, it had slowed enough so she could push hard on the right pedal to make the aircraft pivot. When the aircraft completed a full circle, it came to a halt. Maggie and Greg were staring at a large banyan tree a few feet away.

They unbuckled and reached behind their seats for their M16 automatic weapons.

Bill and Pete untied themselves from the cargo floor. Pete pulled a sawed-off 12 gauge shotgun from its leather sheath and sat it between his legs.

Riley reached for his bag, removing several smoke grenades and two stun grenades. The four team members sat and waited. No one had seen or heard the fighter jet since they landed.

"I think we've seen the last of the fighter," Maggie remarked. "That pilot knows I'm incapable of taking off on such a short runway."

They were trapped.

Maggie turned to Greg and joked, "Well, here's another fine mess you've gotten us into, Ollie."

Greg sat staring out the front windshield, sizing up the banyan tree they came close to plowing into. He looked at Maggie and laughed.

CHAPTER NINE

"Well done, Maggie. You're awesome," Pete called out. "I said you were the best pilot I knew and you just proved it. Once we were below the tree line, how could you see anything? I was freaking out."

Maggie reached to kill the plane's lights. "I couldn't, so I made a guess and guessed right. It was pitch black because clouds had darkened the moon and the landing lights were a little help. And stop bullshitting me about being the best pilot you know. I'm tired of hearing it."

Greg looked at his watch. "It'll be light in an hour. I say we sit tight until we can see better, then make a decision on what to do next. Agreed?" Nods of approval came from everyone. Maggie pulled the last IV from her bag and asked Greg if he would like a cocktail. He laughed and held out his arm. From this point on, the team would have to rely on the small amount of food brought with them for the flight. Bananas, animal crackers, peanut butter, several boxes of raisins and one gallon of water was all that was left.

Pete called out to Greg from the cargo bay, "Duke is

whimpering back here. Does he sense someone near the aircraft?"

Greg smiled, "Nah, he has to pee. Ignore him."

The hour dragged by and no one had much to say. Everyone sensed the urgency and potential danger but didn't want to admit they were terrified of what might lie ahead. For sure, this wasn't expected and now their fate was in the hands of an unknown enemy.

Maggie sat her navigation chart in her lap. "I just checked our position and, by my calculations, we're about twenty miles west of Guantanamo but I'll be damned if I know how to walk there."

Pete responded, "Maggie, can you fly us out of here? The F4 is gone and there's no welcoming party so let's go."

"I told you it can't happen, Pete; the runway is too short. You saw what it took to drop this monster in here. I'm guessing they know we can't fly out, so they figure what's the rush?"

Once the sun reached the top of the tree line, the temperature inside the aircraft began to heat up.

"I've got to pee the dog. Everyone stay put and let me check it out first," Greg said as he released Duke from his leash and opened the large cargo bay door. Hot, humid air poured into the plane. Duke jumped out and raced to the nearby undergrowth to attend to his needs. Greg sat on the edge of the cargo bay with his M16 in his lap, listening for any sounds of human life.

"Maggie, you stay with the aircraft and the rest of us can check out the area," Greg suggested.

The three men stepped to the runway and walked away from the plane. No one spoke. At the opposite end of the runway, the team found a small dirt road hidden by the jungle's overgrowth.

"Okay, this is good. We have a way out. What do you think about packing up what supplies we have and take our chances on this road? We may find our way to Guantanamo," Greg said.

Pete looked at Greg and shook his head. "Cuba is a communist country. If they find us in the jungle with loaded weapons we'll be executed. If we stay with the plane and hide our weapons in the jungle we can tell them we had engine trouble and had to make an emergency landing. They'll search the plane for narcotics and other contraband but when they find nothing, we might be released."

"Pete, you might be right but I may have a better plan. Let's talk with Maggie."

Riley raised his hands over his head and demanded his friends stop giving suggestions. "I haven't had much to say through all of this because I figured you guys are a lot smarter than I am, but have you two forgotten we were forced down by an F4 fighter jet? This is bullshit. We aren't leaving here. Someone or something is going to come and kill us all. So stop with the surrender plans and all the other bullshit about finding Guantanamo. It ain't happening. Personally, if I'm going to die, I want to at least go down in a hail of gunfire. I say we take up our best positions, arm ourselves to the hilt and let 'em bring it on."

Greg put his arm around Bill. "Okay, okay, but let me talk to Maggie first. None of this may be necessary."

The team walked back to the plane and found Maggie pouring over charts.

Greg leaned into the cargo bay and called out, "Maggie, come back here for a second and listen to what we've been discussing."

Maggie climbed from her seat and sat on the edge of the cargo bay.

Greg continued, "We found a road at the end of the runway. We could take that to see where it takes us. Pete thinks we ought to hide our weapons, tell the Cubans we had engine trouble and ask them to release us. Bill has a more pessimistic viewpoint and wants us to entrench ourselves and shoot it out with whomever shows. But I've got another idea and I need your advice. What if we strip down the aircraft and drain all the fuel but a small amount? Then you leave us here and we'll hide in the jungle. Can you get this thing off the ground and fly twenty miles to Guantanamo? Can you do that?"

Maggie pondered Greg's suggestion. It seemed she was always giving the team bad news. After much thought, she spoke. "Oh, baby, thanks for the vote of confidence but we already threw everything out in Fort Lauderdale for that takeoff. This airstrip was probably built by drug smugglers to handle small single engine planes. Maybe if I had a strong head wind, which I don't, and maybe if I didn't have tall trees at either end of the runway, which I do, then maybe, just maybe, I could pull this off. But the bottom line is there is no wind and we do have tall trees at both ends of the runway, so the answer is no. I couldn't make it but thanks for thinking I'm a miracle worker."

Greg spoke, "Well, it doesn't make any difference anyway. Take a look at Duke. I think we're about to have company."

119

Duke had walked twenty feet from the aircraft and was standing in the middle of the runway, staring toward the access road. His tail was motionless and his ears stood straight up. The team heard the faint roar of a truck.

Greg looked at his team. "Everyone hear that? Okay, decision time and I'm calling the shots. Get into the aircraft and let's lock her down."

Without question, the three men jumped into the plane just as two large military trucks turned onto the runway and headed for them.

Duke stood his ground in the center of the airstrip until Greg called to him. "Leave it, Duke. Come on boy, load up. Duke, load up," Greg ordered.

Obedient as always, Duke was the last to jump into the cargo bay.

Maggie closed the cargo door.

"Everyone stay in cargo and I'll go up front and observe," Greg ordered as he crawled into the cockpit. "Damn, I wish we had turned around to face down the runway. I can't see well. Both trucks have stopped and now I see soldiers carrying AK-47's. They're surrounding the aircraft. Don't anyone go crazy and start firing. It's their move. Since we all speak a little Spanish, let's put our heads together on what the hell they're saying."

The soldiers surrounded the aircraft and the team waited for their next move. Ten minutes went by and nothing happened.

Riley spoke, "They're sweating us out. They know how hot it's going to get in here so they'll wait us out."

"I don't think so," Greg responded. "They know we can last a long time in here. For now, let's just wait."

Everyone huddled together in the aircraft and waited, weapons cradled in their arms. Body odor was beginning to permeate the air inside the aircraft. The tension was indescribable. No one spoke. Riley sat staring at the closed bay door as if he thought it might be blown from its hinges at any moment. Minutes passed, then, from the truck's loudspeaker, a voice called out in broken English.

"Attention, Americans. We are aware you're armed. Any hostile action on Cuban soil will be considered an act of war and you'll be eliminated. If you understand, flash your navigation lights."

"Greg, you want me up there with you?" Maggie asked.

"Stay put, I can flash the lights," Greg replied.

Greg reached to turn the lights on and off several times.

The truck's loudspeaker came to life again. "Excellent! You'll now exit your aircraft, one person at a time, with your hands above your head. Any person who exits carrying a weapon will be shot. If you understand this command, flash your lights again. Failure to follow this command will result in your destruction. We'll set fire to your plane."

Greg obeyed, flashing the lights again, and then left the cockpit to join his team sitting in the cargo bay.

Greg shook his head. "We have no options. We can die in this plane or take our chances with the soldiers."

"Bullshit, I didn't sign up to be gunned down by Cuban soldiers on our first mission," Riley blurted. "We have pretty good armament. Let's crank our engines, turn the plane around and taxi into them while blazing away. It's kick-ass time."

Greg shook his head, "Riley, I'm worried you're going to do something crazy like open fire on those soldiers. If you stand your ground, you'll get one shot off before they fire tracers into our fuel tanks, killing us all. If anyone has a thought or idea, now's the time to throw it out."

The team sat in silence.

"Okay, let's hide our weapons in the bottom of the equipment bags. Maggie, you open the cargo bay. We'll leave one at a time. Lock your fingers together above your head. Don't give them a reason to shoot you. Questions, anyone?"

Greg put a leash on Duke and attached it to a cargo tie down.

"You stay here, Duke. Good boy. We'll come back and get you. Good boy. Now lie down."

Maggie opened the bay door and faced six armed soldiers. She put her hands over her head and hopped to the runway, followed by Bill, Pete and Greg. They stood in a row with their hands over their heads. Then they were ordered to walk single file to the rear of the aircraft.

Greg leaned over to whisper to Maggie, "I'll bet Harkin is in hell laughing his ass off at us."

"Silencio! Everyone down on your stomachs; stay still while we search you," the lead guard ordered in broken English.

The team dropped to their knees and then down onto their stomachs. Four soldiers began to search them.

Greg could hear Duke whining and knew he was nervous

because he couldn't see them. As Duke's apprehension grew, he began to bark, softly at first, then louder.

Greg called out, "Leave it, Duke. Leave it."

Duke quieted. A soldier walked up to the bay entrance of the plane and fired two shots into Duke's head, killing him.

"No, no. Not my dog. Don't kill my dog, you son-of-a-bitch!" Greg called out and started to stand. He was struck by a gun butt to his head and knocked unconscious.

Blood trickled from his scalp as he lay on the airstrip. Maggie reached out to him but a soldier stepped on her hand and ordered her to remain in place. She began to cry over Greg's condition and the loss of her dog.

"Greg, are you all right? This is turning to shit," Maggie cried out.

"Silencio, you American bitch. No talking or we'll deal with you the same as your husband," a soldier demanded.

Maggie was shocked. *How would a Cuban soldier know I was Greg's wife?"*

Not having any answers, she closed her eyes and cried. She thought about how good life was for her and Greg in the mountains, even though he was weak and sick. She recalled how Duke had come into their lives nine years ago after becoming lost on the streets of Miami Beach. Duke was just a puppy. She remembered Greg hunted everywhere for the owner and, in the end, said it was just meant to be.

Maggie cried out loud, "Oh, Duke, I'm so sorry we brought you."

She turned her head and was surprised to see Greg was conscious.

"Are you okay, baby?" she whispered.

"I'm okay, it's a scalp wound but what about Duke? Did they kill Duke?" Greg asked, knowing the answer.

"I think so. He hasn't barked since the soldier fired into the plane. All he was doing was barking and you made him stop but they didn't care. Dirty rotten bastards!"

"Will I have to cut out your tongue to silence you?" the angry lead guard asked, staring at Maggie.

The soldiers bound each prisoner's hands in front of their bodies, and then each member was blindfolded and allowed to sit upright on the runway. The sun was rapidly heating the airstrip. Over an hour passed and thirst was setting in. Then they heard the faint roar of a helicopter. The noise of the chopper grew louder. Rotor wash from the chopper brought a comforting breeze and it was obvious it had landed close to where they were sitting.

With the engine still running and the blades whirling at high speed, the captives were lifted to their feet and escorted to the chopper. Two soldiers pulled each team member onto the floor of the bird. Then, without buckling any of them or allowing them to sit, the chopper lifted from the runway. The team didn't know the two soldiers jumped from the chopper, leaving the team unguarded.

Greg shouted over the roar of the chopper. "Maggie, Pete, Bill, are you okay?"

No one responded for fear of being struck or killed. Wind roared through the open bay and Maggie could tell from the noise of the rotor blades they were airborne and moving.

The air grew cool as the chopper rose in altitude and headed toward its destination. Greg moved his body to a sitting position without being stopped. The pain in his stomach was severe and sitting seemed to help. He also knew if he didn't get water soon he would pass out from dehydration. Since his surgery, he needed water often.

Greg's mind wandered, first thinking of his love for Duke and then the attempt on his life. He thought about Pete arriving at their mountain hideaway and how shocked he and Maggie had been to see he wasn't dead. He remembered the bomb shell Pete dropped on him about Mayor Harkin being responsible for his assassination attempt. Then Greg thought, *How could a soldier in the jungles of Cuba know he was married to Maggie? And how did the F4 Phantom find us near the Cayman Trench in the dead of night?* For certain, he regretted pressuring Maggie to be his pilot. He felt he had caused her impending death. Duke would be alive and she would be safely at home if it weren't for his wanting them along. He had insisted Duke accompany them on the mission. Guilt set in and he wanted to tell Maggie how sorry he was but feared he would be struck again if he spoke.

After a short helicopter flight, the blindfolded captives were transferred onto a fixed wing aircraft. Each prisoner was tied to a seat inside the plane. No one was allowed to speak. After a five hour flight, the plane landed and the prisoners were transferred to another helicopter. The flights were well organized with no waiting between transfers.

Each team member knew they were a long way from Cypress and the situation was getting grimmer by the hour.

CHAPTER TEN

When Maggie felt the chopper bank a hard right and start to descend, she tried to calculate how long and how far they had traveled. She had spent countless hours in a cockpit monitoring instruments and was good at judging time. She guessed it had been over four hours, maybe longer. Just as the team felt the impact of the landing, they heard the helicopter's bay doors open. Their blindfolds were removed. The glare of the sun forced everyone to squint. Slowly, the team became accustomed to the bright sun and began to look around. Greg saw he was the only person who had been allowed to sit. Everyone else was lying on their sides.

The Cuban soldiers had been replaced by civilian guards wearing black tank top shirts and military-styled camouflaged pants, bloused at their boots. The guards held AK-47 automatic weapons and ammo belts filled with magazines draped across their shoulders. The team looked around the aircraft and then at each other. Pete was missing.

"Am I permitted to speak?" Greg asked.

"No talking or you'll be shot," was the response.

One by one Greg, Maggie and Bill were helped out of the chopper to an awaiting flatbed truck. Greg noted the jungle was more dense than in Cuba and guessed they were somewhere in South America.

Once they were seated, the leader spoke. His English was excellent and it was obvious he had spent time in the United States. "Welcome to Colombia, my good friends. You'll find water and food in the truck. If you choose to escape, you'll not be pursued. The jungle will eventually take your life. There's no way out so I suggest you enjoy the ride through some of the most beautiful jungles Colombia has to offer. Few Gringos get to see this part of our country."

The leader's grin was sinister and it was obvious he was inviting them to escape. The truck wound its way up a one-lane dirt road in a mountainous area of Colombia. White bellied spider monkeys, hoping for a handout or discarded food, came close to the truck and gawked. The heat was oppressive and, other than a slight breeze from the movement of the truck, the wind was still.

"You know what? Screw it, I'm gonna talk," Bill blurted out. "Where in the hell is Pete and how do we get ourselves out of this shit? I came on this gig to kill dope dealers, not get captured in the first hours of our mission. We need a plan and I would like to suggest...."

At that moment, a single shot rang out. The bullet tore off a chunk of wood six inches from Bill's head.

"Silencio, Gringo! Do not test me," a guard called out.

The shooter was sitting on top of the roof of the truck and had been facing toward the front until he turned and fired a shot toward Bill.

The truck continued to creep along the winding road and eventually stopped at a small creek.

"Get out. We'll walk from here," the lead guard ordered.

Greg dared speak. "What about our water and food? There was no water or food in the truck as you promised."

"Soon, Mr. Predator, soon," was the leader's response.

Greg stared at the guard in disbelief. How did he know his nickname?

With the team's hands still bound with duct tape, they were assisted from the truck and ordered to stand in a straight line.

"You'll cross the river one at a time. The water is knee deep and there are many rocks on the bottom. Once you've crossed, we'll continue, single file, up that steep path. Does everyone understand?" the lead guard asked.

Riley leaned over to whisper to Maggie, "They call that a river? These guys don't get out much, I guess."

"You're either dumb or don't care if you die. I said there is no talking. Do you not understand?" the guard shouted at Riley.

Duct tape was then placed over Riley's mouth.

"All right, I want your attention. Move up that narrow path. Look for snakes along the way and call out if you see one," the leader ordered.

"The only snakes I see are carrying weapons," Greg joked under his breath.

The team started to ascend the steep path. Guards were in the front and rear of the formation. The trek upward was difficult and the team members stumbled several times. Riley found it difficult to breathe through his nose as he made the steep climb. The path was so narrow and the jungle so dense, growth covered the sky above them. Everyone was covered with perspiration - their shirts were soaking wet. Greg noticed, after a half hour of walking, the path widened and became less steep. After several sharp turns, Greg and his team spotted a large mansion in a clearing ahead. They were ordered to stop.

The lead guard spoke, "I've been directed to release your bonds. That's against my judgment, but I must obey. I warn you, at this point in our journey, I've the authority to shoot your kneecaps should you try to run. Are there questions?"

"Yeah, who lives in the mansion?" Maggie asked.

"You'll meet your host soon but for now, everyone sit and we'll provide water for each of you." The guards then cut the duct tape from everyone's hands. They handed cups of water to each team member and when they got to Bill, a guard smiled at him and ripped the duct tape from his mouth, pulling out a huge amount of facial hair. Riley groaned in agony, but refused to give them the satisfaction of yelling out.

As the team sat in the clearing, drinking their water, they spotted a man, dressed in a white linen shirt and pants, leave the house and walk toward them. He was carrying towels and white linen shirts similar to his.

As the man presented the shirts and towels, the lead guard spoke. "My master wants you to be properly attired for your visit. After proper greetings, you'll have dinner with him before getting down to business. Take off your shirts and dry off with the towels, then put on the guest shirts. You can wash your hands once in the house."

"What about me? I'm not wearing a bra. May I step into the jungle to change?" Maggie asked.

The guard laughed, "Do I look stupid? Turn your back and change your shirt. I've seen many tits in my lifetime, some even bigger than yours, Maggie Strong."

Once the team had dried the sweat from their bodies, they put on the white linen Guayabera shirts and were marched single file toward the front entrance to the mansion. A guard opened one of the two large wooden doors to the house. A cool breeze blew across their faces as they walked into the large foyer, decorated with small statues and paintings on both walls.

A decorative fountain was positioned right in front of the foyer separating it from a large empty area just beyond. The sound of the cascading water echoed through the large room. The floors were gray marble and spotless.

"I'll escort you to an area where you can further clean up," the guard said. "If you choose to wash your face, make certain none of the water gets in your eyes or mouth. It is unclean for drinking. Your host has insisted you wash your hands to prepare for dinner."

"Will someone tell me what the hell is going on?" Bill whispered to Greg.

"Beats the shit out of me but I don't think it's good," Greg said. "Don't be fooled with the dinner invitation and all the hospitality. We're prisoners, forced here by a damn fighter jet. I still haven't figured that out yet. We have no choice but to go along but keep an eye on me for signals."

Riley nodded. After cleaning their hands, the captives were led down another corridor to a large, lavishly furnished office. The mahogany desk dominating the room was over eight feet in length. Behind the desk sat a large high-back mahogany chair resembling a throne.

Two walls in the office were filled with large paintings and a third wall contained a mural of a gunman helping an old woman to her feet. In front of the desk, three chairs were situated in a semi-oval fashion.

Greg, Maggie and Bill were escorted to the chairs and ordered to sit. Then they waited. The guards positioned themselves around the office and Greg took a quick count. There were six.

A door behind the desk opened and a small figure appeared. The room had no lighting and that part of the office was away from any windows, making it too dark to see the person who was their host.

The figure remained in the darkness and spoke, "The illustrious Captain Gregory Strong, the infamous Predator. Finally, we meet."

When the man stepped into the light, he smiled, looking directly at Captain Strong. Greg rose from his chair and stared at his host, not smiling or showing emotion. Two armed guards moved toward Greg and stood close to him.

After a moment of silence, Greg spoke. "I was afraid of this. Who else but Pedro Macedo, largest drug smuggler in all of South America, murderer of hundreds, rapist of many young girls and…."

"Please….Captain, I've treated you with respect," Macedo interrupted. "There's no need for name calling. I want you to consider yourself, your beautiful wife and your friend as my guests. Let's stay civil. Sit down, Captain, and let's talk."

Greg knew of Pedro Macedo's reputation although they had never met. He would capture his enemies, toy with them and treat them as guests before he murdered them. It was his Colombian style. Greg knew the three of them would never leave the complex alive.

"Respect, you say? You call killing my dog respect?" Greg asked.

"That was unfortunate. Your dog would have been a nuisance for us, so we were left with little choice. Your dog is at peace. My apologies. I love animals and I've two Dobermans on the premises. We'll keep them leashed for your safety since they don't seem to like gringos," Macedo smiled, looking at each of his three prisoners. "Now, once more, Captain, will you please sit?"

As Greg sat, Maggie reached out to touch his arm with compassion, knowing how upset he was.

"What've you done with Pete Spoto?" Greg asked. "I'm assuming he never left Cuba. Have you killed him?"

"Mr. Spoto is a guest of the Cuban government," Macedo said. "They had issues with him greater than mine. He is no longer my concern. It's how we cooperate with each other. Not like Americans who have this need to piss off everyone. What is it with your President Nixon that he hates us so much?"

Greg ignored the question. He knew Macedo would be forthcoming with information because their death was imminent. Macedo had a reputation of playing this game of being the perfect host with his prisoners until he became bored, then he would murder them. Greg looked at Maggie sitting next to him, her face gripped with fear. Even though she didn't know Macedo's full potential, she knew she might be about to die.

"Your English is better than I expected. I can barely detect an accent. I understand you went to high school in Miami. Is that correct?" Greg asked.

Macedo smiled, pleased that Greg had asked the question. "Four years at Miami High. All my lieutenants speak excellent English also. It is my requirement. It's advantageous for my business that we speak good English." Macedo paused and then continued, "You must also know my mother still lives in Miami. I'm sure you've had her under surveillance."

Changing the subject, Greg asked, "Mr. Macedo, can we make a deal? You may have a great need for my team and what we do," Greg suggested, knowing it was a desperate move.

Macedo leaned back in his desk chair and laughed. "What could a broken down, sick, retired narcotics captain and his illiterate, low life moron friend, have to offer?"

Bill Riley's temper took over. He jumped from his chair and lunged for Macedo. Reacting quickly to the threat, Macedo pulled a pistol from his desk and fired. A small red hole appeared on Riley's forehead as he turned to look at Greg for the last time. Blood oozed from the wound. Greg jumped to his feet and Maggie screamed, placing her hands over her face. Macedo pointed his pistol toward Maggie.

"Sit down, Captain, or your wife will be next," Macedo ordered.

Riley tried to get back to his chair but fell to the floor,

dead. With a snap of Macedo's fingers, two guards dragged Riley's lifeless body from the room.

Macedo spoke in a soft, low tone. "We'll see that he gets a decent burial. We are a civil people. We have a small graveyard just north of the complex where we bury the less fortunate. Please, may I ask you to try to control your temper? Now, what is it that you have to offer me?"

Maggie was crying uncontrollably, her hands still covering her face. Greg asked for permission to console her and Macedo nodded. Greg got up from his chair and leaned down to hold her.

She whispered, "They're going to kill us. I don't want to die." Greg pulled her closer so he could whisper in her ear. "You've got to have faith in me, Maggie. This isn't over yet. I know drug dealers. At the least, I'll negotiate to have them release you. Just keep it together, Maggie, and believe in me."

Maggie's crying slowed and Greg pulled away from her to sit back in his chair. He leaned forward and stared at Macedo, "My team, what's left of it, was contracted by the U.S. government to assassinate drug cartel people. If you free us and make arrangements to have Spoto released, we'll kill your competition and still fulfill our commitment to our government. Don't answer now. Give yourself some time to think about this. It could be a perfect arrangement for all of us."

Maggie, hearing her husband's proposition, stopped crying and held her breath for an answer.

Macedo smiled at his two prisoners. "Ah, finally the moment of truth is here. Backed into a corner like rats, you're willing to sell out and double-cross your government to stay alive. I'm sure your government placed me at the top of your list," Macedo said, pausing to consider the proposal. "I'll think about your proposition but for now, let's talk about my brother. I'm sure you remember him."

"Yeah, I remember him. Is that what this is all about, me killing your brother?" Greg asked.

Macedo, holding his temper, spoke, "Captain, please, if I could correct you. You cornered Jose so he couldn't escape. Then, when he attempted to surrender, you murdered him in cold blood. He was only nineteen years old. He was my only brother and I loved him very much."

Greg raised his index finger and shook it as he spoke. "Pedro, you've left out an important part. Jose was in the process of transporting 300 kilos of cocaine into the United States. I didn't kill him in cold blood. Once we had him trapped, he hesitated and then went for his gun. I had no choice."

"Knowing what a low-life scumbag predator you are, I'm sure you cherished the moment. There is story after story of your ruthless conduct against our people. Your friend, Riley, got what he deserved. He wasn't even smart enough to make it to dinner," Macedo laughed.

Then he snapped his fingers and the guards removed Greg and Maggie from Macedo's office to an adjacent dining room.

The large, polished, mahogany dining table was lavishly decorated. Large bowls containing fresh fruit sat at opposite ends of the table with place settings for twelve. A large vase containing fresh flowers sat in the center of the table.

A moment later, Macedo strolled into his dining room

and confronted his guests. "I'll consider your proposal as it's quite interesting. For now, let's forget about business and enjoy what remains of this day. Please, be seated and allow me to offer you a fine Colombian meal. Our wine is better than anything you've ever tasted."

Macedo sat at the head of the table and offered chairs to Maggie and Greg on either side of him. Once seated, waiters, dressed in white linen, brought hot towels to cleanse their hands. The waiters then presented a small salad containing avocado, mixed greens and thinly sliced strawberries. Maggie looked at the salad, then at Greg and then at Macedo before speaking.

"This is all very attractive, but I can't eat. You've just murdered my friend and minutes later you ask me to eat this. I can't do it." Macedo became annoyed and pulled his pistol from his hip. She held her breath as he slowly laid it on the table in a position within Greg's reach.

"In Colombia, it is considered an insult for a woman to refuse a man's meal. I recommend you eat what is offered you, Senora," Macedo spoke, staring into her eyes.

Maggie picked up her fork, looked at the salad and then at the gun on the table.

"I don't care for avocado but I'll eat the rest to keep you happy." Without looking up, she chewed her salad and struggled to swallow while pushing the avocado to the side. She wondered why her husband hadn't attempted to reach for the gun sitting right in front of him but then realized if he had, the guards would have killed him.

Macedo smiled at Maggie. "A very wise decision, Senora. I hope you both like pork. We have killed our finest pig for this special occasion." Macedo paused, staring at his captives. "Oh, Mr. and Mrs. Strong, I've waited so long for this moment and I want it to be perfect for all of us."

Waiters returned to the table, offering large slices of greasy pork. Both Greg and Maggie took portions for their plates. Then the waiters served wild rice with mushroom.

"Let's enjoy our meal while I tell you about the remainder of your stay with us," Macedo said, smiling.

Again, Maggie tried to contain her emotions and looked to Greg for some sign of encouragement. She was trying not to cry, but was overwhelmed with emotion. The loss of Bill and her dog, coupled with the fact she might be about to die, was too much for her. Seconds passed before Maggie broke down and cried.

"Women...they're so weak," Macedo laughed, holding his wine glass at eye level and out toward Maggie. Then he looked at Greg. "But then again, Mister Predator, they're such treasures, especially a beautiful blossom such as your wife. To find one as beautiful and intelligent as Maggie, who flies airplanes and practices with your S.W.A.T teams, is a rarity. A salute to Maggie Strong, Colombia's woman of the year," Macedo mocked.

Macedo took a large gulp of his wine before sitting the glass on the table. Greg glared at Macedo. This wasn't the first time he had been astounded by things that Macedo knew about their lives. *How could he have learned that Maggie took weapons training with the police department?*

Maggie tried to control her crying and blotted tears with her napkin. "I'm sorry, I miss my dog. Please excuse my conduct," she said, not looking at Macedo but at her husband.

Macedo leaned forward, placing both elbows on the table. "Listen carefully at what I'm about to say for I won't repeat it. I'll sleep on your proposition that we work together to eliminate my competition. You'll have my answer in the morning. In the meantime, be aware I'm going to lock you and your wife in a small room with no windows and one door. Unfortunately, we must turn off our generators at midnight and, except for our refrigeration generators, the complex will be in darkness. There's a candle and matches in your room."

Macedo paused, waiting for his captors to respond. No one spoke for over a minute. Macedo continued. "You'll find your accommodations sparse but clean. Your bed has linens and pillows. With your candle lit, it's the perfect atmosphere for making love together on what might be your last night together. I'm not a barbarian as you've called me so many times."

Greg wanted to show Macedo he was confident his offer would be too generous for Macedo to pass up.

"I'm sure you'll make the right decision, Mr. Macedo. You're a very smart man and didn't get this far by being unwise. I'm much more valuable to you alive than dead. Once I'm dead the government will send another to kill you. As long as I'm alive, you are safe," Greg suggested.

Macedo removed his gun from the table and stuck it in his waistband.

"As I've said, I'll consider your proposal. Now let me give you some bad news. Should I choose not to take your offer, then sometime tomorrow morning, I'll kill you both. So that Maggie can have a restful night's sleep, allow me to tell you about your death," Macedo teased. "With your loving husband tied to a chair in the same room, I'll have you shackled to my bed on your back. Then I'll take my very sharp knife and slowly cut off your clothes, a garment at a time. Do you know how long I've been fantasizing about cutting off your panties and bra?"

Macedo was staring into Maggie's eyes, waiting for a reaction. Maggie looked back at him, stone faced and blurted, "I don't wear a bra, you sick bastard."

"Maggie, knock it off," Greg shouted. "There's a purpose to his bravado. Please try to stay calm."

Macedo laughed, looking directly at Greg as he spoke. "I'm going to have my way with your wife, mister murderer of my brother…Mister SWAT team man…mister drug agent. You're going to sit there in a chair and watch me fuck her until I'm exhausted. Then I might rest awhile and fuck her again, depending on how good she feels when I'm deep inside her. When she's no longer any use to me, I'll place my knife deep into her vagina. When I'm sure I have your full attention, mister big shot asshole policeman, I'll slowly cut her from her pussy all the way to between those beautiful breasts."

Maggie dove from her chair and lunged at Macedo. "You scumbag dope peddler; kill me now!"

She knocked over the large bowl of fruit and several unused wine glasses. Guards rushed forward before she could get to Macedo. Greg sat motionless, his mind working overtime, pondering what to do about their dilemma. The two guards pulled Maggie back to her chair and forced her to sit. They remained on either side of her to prevent further outbursts.

Macedo was angry with Maggie's behavior and it was showing in his speech. "It's unfortunate we have to end this very pleasant evening with such ugliness. Allow me to continue," Macedo said without smiling. "It's a shame Maggie Strong has to die in such a humiliating manner but this is what happens when a beautiful woman marries a murderer and ruthless predator like Captain Strong. It's a shame you'll not be around for your husband's death for I can assure you it'll be more painful than yours."

Macedo pulled a large knife from his boot and showed it to Maggie. "Your husband will die from a thousand cuts to his body with this knife. I'll be careful not to cut any vital areas so the rush of blood will not take his life prematurely. Then, just as I see him start to lose consciousness, I'll cut off his dick and stick it in his mouth. Once he's dead, I'll have photographs taken. Large posters will be mailed to his police department so they can put them on their walls and know what happens to police officers who murder people and use their badge to get away with it."

Macedo laid his knife on the table and pulled the bottle of red wine from its cradle, pouring another glass. Without looking up, he ordered, "Get them out of my sight."

Four guards took Greg and Maggie from the dining room down a long hallway to a door at the end of the corridor. One guard unlocked the door and ordered Greg and Maggie inside. The guards had them remove their linen shirts and handed them their own black shirts. The door was shut behind them. Maggie reached out to Greg to hold him.

"You've got to help me, Greg. I want you to kill me tonight," Maggie pleaded. "I can't chance Macedo will take your offer. I know you can kill me instantly and with little pain. Do it for me, Greg. Don't let me die that horrible death in the morning."

"I will, Maggie, I'll do it in the morning. For now, let's find a way out of this. We have our watches and we know Colombia is close to the same time as Miami, maybe an hour earlier. We have an advantage of knowing time. This may sound weird, Maggie, but I have to rest. I can't sleep but I need to rest. If I don't, I'll be helpless to do anything. I'm exhausted and I'm no longer running on adrenaline."

"No, that's not weird," Maggie answered. "I understand. You rest and I'll have a look around. I'll make note of when the lights go out and I'll set my watch."

Maggie sat on the edge of the bed next to where her husband was lying. She surveyed the room. As Macedo had explained, there were no windows and one door. The room was stuffy and she knew it would get worse as the evening progressed. She gauged the height of the ceiling and guessed it was a little higher than the ceilings in their mountain home, probably twelve feet. The floor was covered with Cuban tile and the walls were concrete. She stared at the small lamp sitting on a table next to the bed.

This must've been a storeroom, she thought as she continued to scan the room. She dropped her head in despair and started to cry. She was ashamed of her behavior and thought she should be stronger than she was. She remembered Greg telling her years ago that pending death brings on a myriad of emotions and one never knows how they'll react until faced with such circumstances. Greg was right.

Maggie lay down next to Greg and thought about her death. She hoped he would have the emotional strength to kill her in the morning. He would probably wait until they heard someone unlocking the door before reaching out to break her neck, snapping her upper vertebra, causing severe spinal shock. It would hurt for a second and then she would be dead.

She stared at the ceiling and pondered her life with Greg. *I'm too damn young to die*, she thought, *but what the hell, this has really turned to shit.* As her eyes scanned the ceiling, they locked on something different in the far corner of the room. Whatever it was, it was covered by the painted ceiling. She quietly slid from the bed, careful not to disturb Greg. *Men are incredible*, she thought as she stared at him sleeping. *The guy is about to die and he's able to sleep. Unbelievable!*

Standing under the section of the ceiling that drew her attention, she could see it was a plate bolted or screwed to the ceiling. She guessed it was about an eighteen inch square. *It's a damn air vent*, she thought, *probably closed a long time ago when Macedo decided this would be his jail.* She looked at her watch as her mind raced.

"Greg, wake up and look at this," Maggie whispered.

Maggie's voice startled him and he jumped up to see why she called. Maggie stood in the far corner of the room, smiling. "Maybe we're outta here, baby. Look at that," Maggie said, pointing to the ceiling.

Greg looked at his watch again. They would lose their electricity in about two hours.

"Looks like a metal plate over an air vent to me. There's so damn much paint on it I can't see how it's attached; maybe screws. Let's hope it's not welded," Greg said with excitement in his voice. "Maggie, listen carefully. I'm going to crouch in the corner of the room and I want you to stand on my shoulders. Use the wall for balance. When you're ready, I'll stand and that should put you right under the plate. See if you can determine how the plate is attached to the ceiling."

"I'm on it," Maggie spoke with enthusiasm, causing Greg to shush her.

Maggie climbed onto Greg's shoulders, using the wall for added balance. "Okay, I'm ready."

Greg rose slowly until he was standing straight.

"Perfect, baby. I can touch it. Give me a minute." Maggie said as she felt the corners of the plate and, even though she couldn't see well, she thought she felt the heads of screws at each corner.

"Hand me a number six screwdriver," she joked.

Greg lowered his wife to the floor.

"I'm certain I felt what could be screw heads on the corners of the plate," Maggie said.

"Okay, we need a hammer and a screwdriver. Let's hope the screws aren't Phillips head," Greg said as he stared at the table lamp next to the bed.

He walked to the lamp and removed the shade. Using the shade holder, he began to unscrew the bulb socket from the lamp base. Underneath, he located the large thin plate holding the socket assembly to the lamp which could be fashioned into a screwdriver.

143

"Light the candle, Maggie. I've got to unplug this lamp for a minute."

Working by candlelight, Greg pulled the felt covering from the base of the lamp and pulled the cord through the thin mounting bracket. Once removed from the lamp, he smiled, holding it up for Maggie to see.

"Give me a second and you can plug this light back in."

He sat the lamp base upright and balanced the light socket on top of the base and then Maggie plugged it back into the wall socket and the lamp lit the room.

Without speaking, Greg flung the mattress and covers from the bed and carried the bed frame toward the corner of the room. It was a crude frame made of heavy wire. The only thing holding the mattress in place was a wire grid fastened to the frame but it would make a perfect ladder. Greg leaned the bed frame against the corner of two walls in an almost upright position.

"Maggie, I need you to hold this bed in place by pushing it hard against the two walls. If I fall, it will make enough noise to alert the guards, so I can't emphasize enough how important it is to keep this bed steady. Are we on the same page?"

Maggie nodded and leaned hard on one side of the wire bed. Greg placed his makeshift screwdriver in his pocket and started his climb. As he stepped onto the wire with one foot, the bed shifted and made a loud noise, scraping on the tile floor. They held their breath, waiting for any outside sounds. Hearing nothing, Greg continued his climb. Once he reached the top of the bed, he lifted one leg over the bed frame and sat on the bed rail. He shifted his body to find a more comfortable position but there was none. Pulling his homemade screwdriver from his pocket, he went to work, scraping at the paint where a bolt might be located.

Maggie leaned hard against the bed and lowered her head in prayer. *Lord, you gotta help us out of this mess,* she whispered to herself.

Greg scraped at the paint for over ten minutes before announcing, "Good news, Maggie, there's a screw flush with the plate. That's why we couldn't see it. More good news, it's a flathead."

Greg continued to scrape at the paint that filled the slot in the screw until it was clean. Shoving his makeshift screwdriver into the slot, he attempted to turn it. It wouldn't move.

"Shit, it must be rusted shut. I can't budge it."

"Want some WD40, baby?" Maggie joked.

Greg was pleased to hear Maggie joke about their plight. He felt so bad he had gotten her into this mess. They both knew he would be forced to kill her in morning if they couldn't find a way out.

"Yeah, baby, toss it up," Greg joked back.

In a desperate effort to try again, Greg placed his screwdriver in the screw's slot and attempted to turn it with all the strength he could muster. Suddenly there was a soft clunk and the head of the screw fell to the floor.

Maggie looked down at the broken screw. "You're right. It was so rusted. You twisted it off."

Greg smiled, "One down, three to go. I have to come down and give my ass a break. What time is it, Maggie?"

"We have one hour before lights out so I recommend you

rest your ass. I've an idea. Let me scrape the paint while you rest. Is that a plan?" Maggie asked.

"Good thinking, Maggie."

Greg handed her the makeshift screwdriver and Maggie climbed the bed. Throwing her leg over the end of the bed, she joked again, "This is not so bad. I must have more cushion in my ass than you."

Maggie began the slow process of scraping the paint from the plate. Paint chips drifted toward the floor as Maggie worked away.

"I'm going great guns here, Greg. I'm going to try to finish scraping all three screws before I come down."

"That would be great, baby. Have at it," Greg responded.

Thirty minutes later Maggie announced, "I've good news. One of the corners has no screw and I've one left. I'm getting good vibes about how this is going, sweetheart."

After another moment, Maggie swung her leg over the bed and started her descent. She handed the tool to her husband and kissed him softly on the lips. "You're up, baby. Good luck up there."

Without response, Greg climbed to the ceiling. He was able to remove the remaining two screws but it was a struggle, fearing he would strip the head of the screws before they would budge. He considered himself fortunate that didn't happen.

"Maggie, if I drop this plate, it's all over for us. This'll have all have been in vain. Drag the mattress over and place it under the bed frame just in case. We might get lucky if I don't drop this damn thing."

Maggie did as Greg instructed while he went to work at removing paint from the sides of the plate.

"If I can get this tool under one corner, I may be able to break the seal and pull the whole thing off," Greg announced without looking away from his work. He continued to work at the plate. Without warning, the plate popped loose from the ceiling and fell, striking Greg's arm. He grabbed for the plate but missed it. It tumbled off his chest and struck the wire bed, sliding toward the mattress below. It struck the mattress hard and fell over, not making a sound. Maggie, holding her breath, stood with her hands to her mouth in horror.

"Steady the bed, Maggie, I'm coming down." Greg whispered.

"Wait, Greg, check out the crawlspace first."

"I can't. I'm exhausted and my ass is killing me. I'm coming down."

As soon as Greg's feet touched the floor, Maggie started the climb without announcing she would check where the opening led.

Midway up, Greg called to her, "Wait, Maggie, you'll need a candle and matches."

Maggie leaned down to reach for them, smiling at Greg. It was obvious Maggie had new hope they would find a way out. Once she straddled the top bed rail, she reached up into the opening and laid the candle and matches at its edge. Holding onto the sides of the opening, she pulled herself up until her feet were standing on the top of the bedrail.

As she lifted herself into the opening, Greg noticed the muscular tone of her biceps as she pushed herself into the hole. He was proud she had maintained her physical fitness throughout their years together.

Maggie lit the candle and started her crawl through the shaft. She moved slowly as the candle provided little light for what lay ahead. After moving into the shaft ten feet, she came to a dead end. A plate had been welded in place across the shaft. Hope drained from her as she crawled backward toward the opening.

Remaining silent, she lowered herself to the top of the bed rail, blew out the candle and started to descend the bed. She turned, saying nothing to Greg and dropped the candle and matches to him. As she took the next step, the light went out in their room and she stood in total darkness. The generators had shut down.

"Don't move, Maggie. Let me get the candle lit," Greg instructed.

He sat the lit candle on the small table and returned to the bed to support it while Maggie continued her descent. Once she reached the floor, she turned to embrace Greg.

"The damn thing is welded shut. We have no way out. We're screwed," she cried.

Greg held her. "We'll find a way, Maggie. I need time to think."

They sat on the floor with their backs against the wall, staring at the door at the opposite side of the room where guards would enter in the morning. Maggie wrapped her arm around Greg's arm and scooted as close to him as possible. The candle burned steadily and Maggie marveled at how much light one little candle could produce. She thought, *if it wasn't for our plight, this would be romantic.* She chuckled under her breath at the irony of that thought.

She leaned closer to Greg and whispered, "You know what? I would rather die like this...together...than have lived the way we were. I don't know how much longer I could've lived seeing you so depressed, day after day. At least now you're the old Greg and full of life. Maybe not as strong but at least your head is straight."

She laid her head on his shoulder. He leaned forward and kissed her lips hard and long. For the next fifteen minutes, the two sat in silence. Maggie knew how important it was for her to remain silent and give him time to think. In reality, she knew there was no hope for either of them. In the morning, they would hear the door unlock, Greg would reach to hold her tight, then, in an instant, break her neck, killing her.

"Okay, we're outta here," Greg blurted, surprising Maggie. "I've a plan. Listen to me and critique this scenario. Tell me where I'm wrong. Macedo will not come here in the morning with his guards. He'll have them bring us to where he is. The guards don't know the shaft is welded shut. I'm betting it's an old weld and Macedo never told anyone about it. Why would he?"

"So what?" Maggie asked, not fully understanding what Greg was thinking.

Greg turned and grabbed her shoulders. "So what, you ask? So what if we stage an escape. We'll make it look like we've gotten out through the shaft. When they run to get Macedo, we'll make our escape."

Maggie stared into Greg's eyes and saw the hope.

"You want me to punch holes in the plan, right?" Maggie

asked. "Where are we going to hide in this tiny room? We can't hide in the shaft because the guards will return with Macedo before we could get out. Maybe if we hung from the opening and dropped to the floor one at a time, but that takes time. If Macedo is close, we won't make it. What if one guard stays behind while the others go for Macedo? What if they lock the door as they leave? Lots of if's, Greg, lots of if's."

"Good thinking, Maggie. I need that. Now hear me out. We won't hide in the shaft. We'll tie bed sheets together and make it look like we climbed the sheets into the shaft and made our escape. Now don't laugh, Maggie, we'll hide under the bed. We're not dealing with Albert Einstein brains here. The guards will come into the room, see the plate has been removed from the ceiling and see the sheets tied together. They'll panic and run for Macedo. They won't search the room. If they leave a guard behind, I'll try to use the element of surprise and push the bed at him to overpower him. If he kills us, that's where we were heading anyway. If they lock the door behind them, we are screwed, but I don't think, in a state of panic, they'll think to do that. Why lock a room with no one in it? They know Macedo will be so enraged, they might be killed themselves at allowing us to escape. They'll act out of fear."

Maggie sat silent for a moment, going over the plan in her head before speaking. "There's no place in the shaft to tie the sheet. How do we pull that off?"

"I thought of that," Greg countered. "Again, I'm betting the guards don't know there's no place to tie the sheet. We'll thread the end of the sheet into the bolt hole in the plate and lay it up in the shaft. Remember, we're not dealing with smart people. These idiots were working the coca fields before this assignment. When they enter in the morning, the hanging sheet will be all they can see. They'll run from the room. I just know it. Maggie, you've got to believe in this plan. What do ya think?"

Maggie rose to her feet and faced her husband still sitting on the floor. "Well, you better get off your dead ass and get to work, Captain."

Greg smiled and jumped up. The two bed sheets, lying in the corner of the room, were tied together. The end corner of the sheet was threaded through the bolt hole in the plate and tied. Using the sheet as a rope, Greg held it over his head to see if it would hold the weight of the plate. Continuing to hold the sheet over his head as the plate pivoted, Greg turned to Maggie. "Okay, pilot lady, we're in business."

He put the opposite end of the sheet through his belt loop and started to climb the bed frame. After throwing a leg over the top bed rail, he untied the sheet from his belt loop and pulled the plate to him. He then fitted the plate through the opening diagonally and sat it well out of sight in the shaft. He looked down at Maggie, giving her a thumbs up. *Damn, this is a plan*, he thought as he smiled at her. The bed sheet hung from the opening and almost touched the floor.

Once back on the ground, Greg hugged Maggie. "This is going to work, baby. Just walk over to the door and look at what a great visual effect they'll get when the guards walk in here. It looks like we've escaped. Now we have to sleep so we can be alert for tomorrow."

Maggie knew there were even more scenarios she could

bring up to show the plan could fail but decided to keep quiet since there was little either of them could do about it.

"Did you say sleep? You gotta be kidding. You expect me to sleep knowing what may happen in the morning?" Maggie asked.

"Then rest, Maggie. Close your eyes and it might happen. At least try it."

Maggie nodded and the two of them pulled the bed from the corner of the room and repositioned it to its original place. They placed the mattress on the bed and while Greg stood by the door, Maggie slid under the bed to get the effect of what the guards would see in the morning.

"Not good, Maggie, I can see you from where I'm standing. Move the bed diagonal to the entrance," Greg instructed.

Maggie crawled from under the bed and did as instructed.

"That's perfect. We'll sleep on the mattress until about five and then move underneath. Is that good?" Greg asked.

Maggie didn't respond but laid down on the mattress and closed her eyes.

"Blow out the candle and I'll see you in the morning," she whispered to her husband.

Walking to the bed, Greg sat and blew out the candle. The room became pitch black. He reached out for his wife and cuddled next to her. Neither of them spoke. As was usually the case, Greg fell asleep after a moment. It took Maggie an hour to fall into a light, restless sleep.

CHAPTER ELEVEN

"Good morning, Senor Spoto….wake up….It's time to wake up."

The crumpled man, lying in the fetal position on the floor of the dimly lit room, didn't move. A uniformed guard was ordered to lift him to a small chair in front of a desk. Pete Spoto sat, semiconscious, trying to focus on the man behind the desk. Spoto had been brutally beaten. Large purple bruises covered his cheeks and forehead. One eye was swollen shut.

Raul Castro carefully unbuttoned the top pocket of his starched khaki shirt and lifted its flap. Pulling out an unwrapped cigar, he smelled its aroma for a few seconds before placing it to his tongue, then began wetting it by rolling it over his lips. Pulling a small cutter from his pants' pocket, he clipped the end of his smoke and lit it. He leaned back in his chair and drew smoke into his lungs while staring at the man sitting in front of him. He leaned forward and blew smoke into Pete's face.

"Good morning, Senor Spoto. Look at me so I'll know

you're awake. At this moment it's seven in the morning at the Macedo compound and I must assume your three friends have been executed by now. I wish to personally congratulate you and thank you for delivering them to Macedo for me. Your plan was superb."

Spoto, now more awake, tried to fight through a severe headache and communicate with his captor. "You piece of shit! What is this, a typical Cuban double-cross? I held my end of the bargain and for that you have your thugs beat me and lock me in a cell. I would expect more from the Defense Minister of Cuba. Even your brother wouldn't sink this low."

Raul Castro smiled at his victim. "You Americans are so stupid. Maybe naïve is a better word. To begin, never insult a man who has the power to kill you. Did you think I would allow you to get away with this because you delivered your friends to Macedo? You must know how close Macedo and I are and how close we work with the Colombian government. How else does one get a Colombian purchased American made F4 fighter jet to escort you to my jail? You're a fool."

"I did my part. I demand you release me...now!" Spoto replied.

Raul Castro smiled at his prisoner. "You're in no position to make demands. Would you like a cigar, Senor Spoto? It's an exquisite smoke."

Castro pulled another cigar from his pocket and held it out to Spoto who sat motionless while glaring back with his one good eye.

"You were handsomely paid for your delivery, Senor

Spoto, as were your comrades," Castro responded, placing the cigar back in his pocket.

"Comrades; I don't have comrades. Communists have comrades. They were once my friends and what good is the money if you're going to kill me?" Spoto said bitterly.

Castro reared back in his chair and laughed. "Excellent point but this is not about the money, it's about revenge. The money we gave you and your comrades is chicken-shit money. As you Americans like to say, it's time to pay the piper."

Castro took a long drag of his cigar and hesitated before speaking again. "Our intelligence is much better than you Americans give us credit for. We know that in December of 1971 one of President Nixon's unmarked government Cigarette boats intercepted a forty-four foot trawler in the Florida Straits. Without provocation, government agents stood on the bow of their boat and emptied their automatic weapons into the hull of our trawler. It eventually sunk. We lost six comrades that evening and two of them were my friends."

Spoto jumped from his chair to speak but a guard placed a garrotte around his neck and forced him to sit.

"I had nothing to do with any of that," Spoto replied. "I was in Panama in December of '71. Your intelligence about me being on that Cigarette is flawed. Now let me go. Besides, I still have many friends with DEA. Release me and I'll find out who the agents were that night. I'll tell you who led the command. Even better, I'll help you set them up for capture, just as I did with Captain Strong."

Castro laughed at his prisoner, "You're a bigger whore than even I could've imagined. You're also very stupid. In early December you were not in Panama because you made credit card charges in Miami. We know you used your credit card at Dania Jai-alai the night before the incident with our trawler, you piece of shit."

Momentarily speechless, Pete dropped his head to try to ease his pounding headache. He spoke. "There were two thousand kilos of marijuana and a hundred kilos of cocaine on that boat. When we approached it, they fired first. What were we to do? We kept firing as long as they kept firing. Then it was all over and the boat was sinking. I was doing my job."

"Helpless sailors on a fishing trawler were no match for the speed and weaponry of your agents. Those sailors were armed with handguns," Castro replied angrily. "Our sailors would have never opened fire against such odds. No, Senor Spoto, they surrendered. You boarded the boat, found the drugs and then sunk it. Our sailors were left at sea to perish but one grabbed a life vest and we found him three days later, twenty two miles from Key West. That sailor had no reason to lie and he told us the truth. You're lying again."

Pete sat speechless. His mind raced as he tried to think of a bargaining chip he could use to save his life.

Castro knew he had pinned Spoto into a corner and was reveling at the thought of having the upper hand. Again, he pulled a cigar from his pocket and held it out to Spoto. "I insist you smoke with me. I'll light it for you."

"I'd rather light my own. Thank you anyway," Spoto responded.

Ignoring Spoto's request, he held out his burning lighter.

Spoto bit the end of the cigar and spit it on the floor. He leaned forward, allowing Castro to light his smoke.

Castro asked, "Tell me about the assassination blunder on Captain Strong. What happened?"

Spoto took a deep draw from the cigar but didn't inhale. As he spoke, the smoke drifted from his mouth. "What happened, you ask? What happened is Harkin is an idiot. He hired some amateur, a Canuck dying of cancer, who wanted to set up his ailing mother with cash before he packed it in. Stupid, stupid, stupid! The guy couldn't even kill Strong with a 12 gauge shotgun at point blank range; stupid, stupid, stupid. When Macedo heard of the blunder, he devised his own plan to kill Strong. That's when you got involved."

Castro leaned forward on his elbows and frowned at Spoto. "You must know, Senor Spoto, I'm never going to let you leave this island alive. You're a snake. Tell me what I want to know and I may decide not to kill you. Living in a cell for the rest of your life would be better than death, don't you agree?"

"I've a better offer for you, Mr. Castro. Give me a bottle of aspirin and I'll tell you what you want to know. You spent years in a Cuban cell under Batista. You tell me, would it be better if I were dead?"

Castro rose from his chair and walked around his desk to approach Spoto from behind. Pete closed his eyes and cringed. He knew of Raul's reputation. Castro loved to have friendly conversations with his prisoners, then walk up, pull his pistol from his holster and shoot them in the back of the head. Pete kept his eyes closed and awaited his death.

"Bring the man a bottle of aspirin," Raul called to a

guard. "The leaders of Cuba believe death is a void, as before you were born. Not good… and not bad. It's just nothing. Killing you would be too good for you. No, I want you to rot in prison for the rest of your life. Now tell me, why would the Director of DEA, the illustrious Mr. Levinson, fake your death and give you a face change? What was your assignment then? I want details."

"Are you going to shoot me after our conversation is over?" Spoto asked.

"What, you don't believe what I said? Please, Agent Spoto, I can shoot you at anytime but I'm an honorable man. If you please me with information, I'll make life more comfortable for you in prison. If you lie, you'll eat food from the dirt and live in chains for the remainder of your life. Is that fair, my friend?"

For the first time since being lifted to his chair, Pete began to focus with his one eye. He realized he wasn't sitting in an office but in an interrogation room at the jail. The dimly lit room offered no comforts and by turning in his chair, he could see one door and four unarmed guards standing near it. Spoto looked down and realized he had urinated in his pants. He looked up at Castro and spoke. "Well, that's not so comforting. My fear is when you hear the simple truth, you'll be angry with my explanation and kill me. You must give me time to explain. Is that fair?"

Castro reached out and snatched Pete's cigar from his hand.

"You're wasting a good cigar. You're not smoking it; you're toying with it like you're toying with me." After snatching the cigar from Pete's hand, he cut the wet end of the smoke with his cutter. He offered the lit cigar to a guard.

"You've little choice. You can only hope I believe you. You're in no position to bargain." Castro said, losing patience with his prisoner.

Castro returned to his chair behind his desk. "Well, Mr. Special Agent, what's your response?"

Spoto hesitated, trying to get his thoughts together. "I got drunk and injured a very prominent woman and her daughter while driving a government issued car in Miami. There were serious civil liabilities involved. The woman's husband is a law partner in one of the biggest civil litigation firms in Miami. DEA was going to shell out a lot of money because of my mistake. So they fired me but had to re-hire me when Nixon wanted to give me an award."

Castro started laughing loudly. "Why didn't they tell Nixon you had been fired? Have they no balls? What did you do to impress the President of the United States? Now I've many questions. This is good for you, Senor Spoto. Tell me more."

"I'm afraid to tell you. Then again, I'm afraid not to tell you," Spoto said before responding. "It was over that Panama cocaine deal that occurred when I was working down there. You must know about it. It was in all the American papers. It was a huge catch for DEA."

Castro seemed pleased with his prisoner. "Bring this man something to eat and drink," he called to a guard. "I don't like these hostilities, Agent Spoto. When someone pleases me, I give rewards. When I'm not pleased...well, you know what happens. Tell me more. How did you and Macedo get hooked up?"

Spoto became hopeful, seeing he was pleasing Castro. "That's when things got more complicated. Unrelated to anything I was doing in Panama, the Miami Beach mayor wanted Captain Strong killed. Strong was at the brink of putting the mayor's kid in jail for ordering their housekeeper killed. The mayor's kid had knocked her up. They were being blackmailed by the housekeeper so they killed her. Then the mayor hired an amateur to assassinate Strong. The rest is history."

"No, no, Mr. Spoto, the rest is not history. How did you hook up with Macedo?" Raul asked.

Spoto could see he was continuing to please Castro. In hopes of getting himself freed, he continued. "I was approached by two of Macedo's lackeys while eating one evening in a Panama City restaurant. They took me to Macedo's car outside the restaurant. Macedo knew DEA might fire me at anytime so he offered me a job."

Castro interrupted, "Pedro Macedo offered you a job? What balls this man has! What a risk Macedo took! You could have gone to DEA with that information and double-crossed him."

Spoto laughed, "Nah, I was done with DEA. I was offered $200,000 in advance to bring Greg Strong to Macedo's mansion. I took the offer and then talked Levinson into allowing me to retire. He came up with the face change and funeral to save his ass in the civil case against DEA. I agreed. I made up the Nixon story, used the information I had on Harkin to get them to fly to the Cayman Trench. I gave Greg and Maggie Strong $200,000 each of Macedo's money to get them on the team. The timing was perfect. Like you said before, that's chicken shit money in the drug world. What I didn't count on was you turning on me."

Pete began to feel better about his standing with Castro. He looked around the large interrogation room to determine if an escape was possible and then continued. "That piece of shit Harkin took a swim and I handed up Strong to Macedo."

Castro laughed, "A small agreement between Macedo and me you weren't aware of. Macedo had the connections with his government to supply the military jet and, in return, I have you as a guest in my prison."

A guard walked into the interrogation room and sat a large plate of black beans and rice in front of Spoto. He reached for the large tin cup filled with water that accompanied the food and drank until it was empty. He stared at the food but didn't eat. "Can I have more water?"

Castro shook his head, "You might get a mild case of diarrhea from the water you just drank, but you'll survive. In fact, you have pleased me, Senor Spoto. I'll allow you to live in a cell and not be shackled...for now. We'll talk again soon. I want to speak with Macedo first. Eat your food."

Spoto picked up a fork and shoveled the food into this mouth. He didn't realize how hungry he was until he took the first bite. It pleased Castro that his prisoner was eating.

"Bring this man a cold beer. Do you like Russian beer, Mr. Spoto?"

"Never tried it but there's a first time for everything,"

Pete said, now happy that he and Castro were on better terms.

When the guard returned with the beer, he whispered into Castro's ear. Castro was displeased at what he had heard and jumped to his feet. "Take the prisoner to his cell."

"Can I take the beer with me?" Spoto asked.

Castro reached out in anger and swatted the beer from the table and it spilled on the floor as the can slid across the room.

"I take it that means no," Spoto responded.

Castro stormed from the interrogation room while two guards escorted Pete back to his cell. Once outside the prison walls, Castro walked to a nearby car and got into the back seat. "Don't just sit there, talk. Tell me the message is not true."

Raul Castro's secretary was a military captain and devoutly loyal to the regime. He was also aware of Castro's temper and knew he had to treat the situation with care. As he handed his boss a small piece of paper, he spoke.

"Sir, this just came in on our coded wire service. It has not been verified. I was reluctant to use the phone for verification on a matter such as this so I brought it to you. Do you want me to make a call?"

Castro stared at the piece of paper and read the words over and over in disbelief. *One dead. Husband and wife now working with us. Do not eliminate your prisoner.* He wadded the paper and threw it to the floor.

"Is everyone a damn whore?" Castro shrieked. "He's working with Strong? No, don't make a call. The CIA listens to all calls between Cuba and Colombia. Get my chopper ready. I'll make a personal visit to Macedo. He has gone mad. Macedo and Strong are working together? For this behavior, I'll use Macedo's mother as a stool to fuck a cow. Take me to the airport."

CHAPTER TWELVE

Maggie woke from her light sleep. Adrenaline poured through her. She could hear talking outside their door. She woke Greg and whispered in his ear, "I think it's time. God, I'm so scared."

"Initiate the plan, baby. Stay in control. If we stick with the plan, you'll be fine," Greg assured her.

In complete darkness, they quietly slid from their bed and crawled underneath it. Maggie pulled the blanket down to the floor so it would hide them. She groped in darkness, trying to feel if the blanket concealed them. They could hear loud voices, then a key in the door. Greg pulled Maggie closer and held her. Maggie and Greg closed their eyes so as not to be blinded by daylight. They both knew if Macedo was with the guards, the stunt wouldn't work. Greg would have to kill his wife the instant they were detected. He was in perfect position to break her neck from their prone position.

Greg moved the corner of the blanket that covered the side of the bed so he could see part of the room, keeping one eye closed. He prayed. *Lord, I never bother you for much, but I could use a little help right about now.*

Greg saw four guards enter the room carrying weapons. The guards saw the empty bed and the sheets tied together that hung from the opening in the ceiling.

"They've escaped through an air vent," a guard announced in Spanish. "Do not inform Macedo."

Three of the guards dashed from the room but one guard hesitated at the door to take one last look. He walked slowly to the empty bed and poked at the blanket on the floor. "Ay Dios mio!" he muttered under his breath as he walked from the room, leaving the door open.

Greg and Maggie slid from under the bed and stood on each side of the open door. Time wasn't on their side. The guards assigned to watch the room knew they would be held responsible for the escape. They had run from the room in an attempt to find the prisoners before they had to tell their boss. They also realized they might be murdered for their mistake.

Greg took a quick look into the empty corridor.

"Grab the candle and matches from the table. Let's move! Stay glued to me, Maggie. If I get hit, run. Make them shoot you," Greg ordered.

It was uncanny how quiet it was in the complex. Greg thought it would be much noisier with orders being shouted and people running through the hallways as news of the escape spread through the complex Then it dawned on him the four guards were too afraid to tell Macedo of the escape. They were out trying to find them on their own. Assuming the escapees would leave the building, the guards were probably outside the compound looking for them.

Greg and Maggie ran down the corridor, turning right at its end. This led them back into the dining room where Macedo had sealed their fate. Finding the room empty, they raced toward a doorway they surmised led to the kitchen since all the food came from that direction. When they pushed open the kitchen's swinging doors, they came face to face with an armed guard. Without hesitation, Greg rammed the heel of his hand just underneath the surprised guard's nose, breaking the cartilage and driving it into his brain. He was dead instantly.

After removing the AK-47 from the guard's shoulder, the two slid along the kitchen wall until they entered a food storage room.

"This isn't good, Maggie. I would rather have stolen a weapon than have killed a guard to get it but this will have to do," Greg said. "If they find the guard they'll know we're armed. I'm hoping they'll assume we left the premises through the kitchen. The safest place for us right now is somewhere inside this house."

Greg looked out the kitchen window. There was no activity around the premises.

"At some point those four guards will have to alert Macedo of our escape and this compound will be teaming with guards," Greg whispered. "I'm hoping they'll think we have escaped into the jungle and will concentrate their efforts there. We need a place to sit tight, maybe even for two days. Let's grab some food. Bread and water will be good. God,

I wish Pete were with us. I could use his smarts right now," Greg said.

As the two scoured the food storage room for food, they heard the generators kick on, providing electricity to the compound.

"Have you forgotten about the dogs?" Maggie asked. "They'll sniff us out. And how in the hell are we going to get out of Colombia when we can't even get out of this house? Do you know how much jungle there is between us and our freedom?"

"One issue at a time, babe," Greg responded. "If the dogs find us then that's it for us. If our scent is weak, we might get lucky. I haven't figured out the rest yet. I need time. I'm not even proficient with this weapon. But first we have to find a place to hide."

"Well, we can't stay here. This is where the food is prepared and I'm surprised there are no cooks here yet," Maggie said as she shoved rolls into the pockets of her black cargo pants. Maggie pointed, "Where does that small door in the corner lead to?"

"Don't know, I've never been invited here before," Greg wisecracked.

Greg dropped to his knees and tugged at the small door, only four feet high and two feet wide. He gazed into the dark opening.

"I see stairs, Maggie. You still have the candle and matches?"

Maggie reached down to hand Greg the matches. Holding a lit match over his head, he slowly crept down the stairs. After a moment of quiet, Greg returned to the storage room.

"It's the bastard's wine cellar," Greg whispered. "We'll have to hope Macedo is not in a wine drinking mood with two prisoners on the loose. I think we've found our new home. If you're nice, I'll even treat you to a glass of vino," Greg joked. "Help me drag the guard to the stairs. He'll be our guest for a while."

Maggie shook her head in disapproval. "No, he'll start to smell by tomorrow and in that confined cellar, it will be horrible."

Greg grabbed the guard by the collar and dragged him toward the cellar. "We have no choice. If they find the body in the kitchen, they'll concentrate their search in this area and we'll be found."

Maggie didn't argue. *This was no time to debate*, she thought. She grabbed the guard by the top of his shirt and the two of them pulled him to the stairs.

"Grab his legs, Maggie."

The corpse was pulled down the stairs and Maggie closed the cellar door behind her.

Greg lit the candle. "Now we sit and wait. Help me hide him under the stairs."

The guard was placed in such a position that anyone looking down the stairs from the storage room couldn't see him.

"Maggie, we'll position ourselves in that far corner. For now, let's leave the candle on. I need to figure out this weapon. We have six matches left. We'll only light the candle when necessary. We'll eliminate our body waste under the stairs next to the guard. Are we on the same page, baby?"

Maggie nodded and then asked, "Do you have a plan? I mean here we are sitting in a damn wine cellar in the middle of Colombia's thickest jungles, surrounded by armed cartel thugs who probably have orders to shoot us on sight."

Greg reached out to hug her. "I would be lying to you if I told you I've a plan. For now, we need to sit here and let the search wane until Macedo is sure we have run into the jungle. Maybe then he'll consider us dead and we can make our move. What move that will be is uncertain. I know there are horses somewhere close. It's how they get to and from the coca fields."

"You smell like a goat, Greg," Maggie joked.

Maggie pushed herself from him and asked, "Horses, you say? I've never ridden a horse. I guess I can learn fast if that's the only way out of this."

Greg didn't respond. He studied the AK-47, cocking, ejecting and reloading its ammo. He pointed the weapon several times, familiarizing himself with the sights.

"Let me show you this weapon, Maggie, just in case I go down. You'll take the weapon and use it. Remember, you're a good shot."

Greg held out the weapon for Maggie to take. She folded her arms, unable to conceive of her husband being dead. Then she reconsidered and took it. "I know how to aim and pull a trigger. Just show me where the safety is and how to clear a jam."

Maggie reached for her husband's hand. "If you're hit, Greg, I'll take the gun and kill myself. I cannot fight an entire cadre of drug smugglers. I'll deny Macedo his pleasure of having me. You know I'll do that, don't you, babe?"

Greg leaned forward and blew out the candle. Wanting to change the subject, he asked, "How many sea urchins do you think are wrapped around Harkin right now, eating his flesh? Wadayathink, a thousand or more?"

Maggie smiled, "That's not something I want to think about right now but if my studies on the matter are correct, there'll be nothing left of him in a month. Yuck, let's change the subject. I don't want to hear his name again. God, it's dark in here. Hold me, please," Maggie asked.

"I thought I smelled like a goat?" Greg responded.

"I'll hold my nose. Hold me, damn it."

Greg and Maggie sat huddled together. An hour later there was much shouting and cursing both inside and outside the mansion. It was obvious the guards had informed Macedo of the escape.

CHAPTER THIRTEEN

Raul Castro's helicopter positioned itself over the open field that had been cleared as a landing sight for Macedo's chopper. It was the same clearing where Bill, Greg and Maggie had landed earlier. Macedo's chopper sat tied down at one corner of the field.

The pilot positioned his aircraft so his rotor blades would barely miss the parked helicopter. Once on the ground, the rotor blades slowly came to a stop. When the dust and loose debris settled, Castro opened the chopper door and stood with his arms folded. It was obvious from his frown he was still angry.

Macedo and four of his guards had been sitting on horses nearby, hidden from the landing site by heavy foliage. When they appeared into the opening, Castro gave them a broad smile and walked toward Macedo who dismounted. The two men walked toward each other and hugged.

Macedo released his grip on Castro and spoke. "Welcome back to Colombia, old friend. I'm surprised by your sudden visit but you're always welcome here. I've brought extra horses for you and your guards. I welcome you to my home. I hope your stay will be long and pleasant."

Castro smiled, showing pleasure at the invitation. "Comrade, it is unfortunate I cannot take you up on your generous offer, but my visit, while important, must be kept short. I've flown all this distance to avoid the telephone and to protest you accepting the American dogs as your allies. This man killed your brother. I take this as an insult. I demand an explanation."

Macedo placed his hand over his heart, a sign he would be speaking from his soul. "Comrade Castro, I must tell you I lied in my communiqué. I was ashamed to tell you that Strong and his wife have escaped. They will be captured soon, I'm sure. They cannot get far in these jungles. I sent you the message hoping you had not eliminated Spoto. We may still need him. Riley is dead."

Castro looked disturbed. "I don't give a damn about Riley. I have Spoto in my cell and I thought Strong would be dead by now. How could you be so careless?"

"Please accept my deepest apologies. Strong tricked my guards into believing he had escaped by tying ...

"Enough," Castro interrupted, "I don't want to hear about how stupid your guards are. How many of my soldiers would you like to expedite the search? What about your dogs? Are they on the hunt?"

"Thank you for your kind offer. My dogs are not well trained and get little practice. They're attack dogs but otherwise useless. And may I remind you if any of your soldiers are seen on Colombian soil, it can have major repercussions between me and my government," Macedo warned.

172

"You're a fool. Take my offer. Besides this is not your government," Castro reminded Macedo. "You're Argentinean and have you forgotten I've major issues with Strong myself? I wanted him dead as much as you. We cannot allow him to escape."

Again, not wanting to offend Castro, Macedo placed his hand over his heart and spoke. "He will not escape my country, Commander Castro, this is a delicate situation. My coca fields thrive because the Colombian government does nothing to interrupt their growth. I pay a lot of people for that favor. But Cuban soldiers traipsing through our jungles will cause me problems. Be a good friend and let me handle this."

"As you wish, comrade; send a coded message when Strong is dead. I assume you have orders to shoot on sight."

Macedo nodded. Castro turned without the usual farewells and boarded his chopper. As the chopper blades began to rotate, Macedo climbed onto his horse and spoke with a guard.

"Pull the peasants from the fields and expand your search. I want them both dead before nightfall."

***

Within an hour, hundreds of workers fanned out across the dense jungle surrounding the mansion and began the search while Greg and Maggie sat quietly in Macedo's wine cellar under the floor of his kitchen.

When Macedo returned to his house, he entered the storage room where Greg and Maggie had been kept. Sitting on their bed, he stared at the bed sheet hanging from the vent hole in the roof. He thought, *damn, they were here when the guards came. My guards turned them loose when they left the door open. How could they be so stupid? How could I be so stupid? Why didn't I go with them this morning? I should have known better.*

Macedo dropped his head and closed his eyes. He was angry with himself and disappointed his captives had outsmarted him.

Think, damn it, Macedo pondered. *I've got to think like Strong thinks. Where would he run to? Where would he hide? He knows there's no escape from these jungles.*

Macedo rose to his feet and walked to the door. He ordered two guards to take automatic weapons and guard the helicopter. As they turned to leave, Macedo called to them. "That's his plan. The woman will try to fly out of here. There's no other way for them to escape. On second thought, take two others with you. Stay there until you're relieved. Do not, under any circumstances, leave the helicopter. Do you understand?"

The guards nodded.

***

Nightfall came and the search had to be called off. The four guards guarding the helicopter were relieved. They would sleep in shifts. At midnight the generators shut down and Macedo lay in his bed unable to sleep. It would be a long night. He felt frustrated.

Greg and Maggie sat in darkness in the back corner of Macedo's dirt floor wine cellar. He held her in his arms as she tried to sleep. He dosed off several times during

174

the night but woke with a start when he thought he heard noises. Maggie fell into a deep sleep. Her head slid from his shoulder to his lap. He kept his hand on her while fingering the automatic weapon lying next to him with his other hand.

***

The next morning, Greg and Maggie were awakened by the sound of the generators starting up.

"We gotta eat, Maggie," Greg told her, lighting the candle and reaching for a roll taken from the kitchen.

"Careful, Greg, the wheat will play havoc on your digestive track. Small bites and chew it well," Maggie ordered.

"Yes, Mommy," Greg joked. "Can you smell the guard? He'll be even riper by tonight. If anyone comes in here for wine, they'll smell the guard and we're done for. Let's hope Macedo is not in a wine drinking mood."

Maggie pulled off a chunk of roll with her teeth and chewed. "Tell me your plan. I know you have one. I know you have a way out of here although I can't imagine what it is. If it involves horses, may I suggest two in a saddle? I don't know how to ride and I'd be more of a hindrance than anything."

"Forget the horses," Greg spoke. "They're useless in the dense jungle. They use them to ride to the fields. Other than that, they're good for nothing."

Relieved she wouldn't have to mount a horse, she asked, "Well, baby, I'm waiting. What's the plan?"

Greg looked straight into Maggie's eyes. "You're flying us out of here tonight. In darkness we'll make our move. We'll sneak into the kitchen and pick up more bread and another

175

bottle of water. By 2 AM, this place will be sound asleep and most of the guards will have given up hope we'll ever be captured. We'll leave by the kitchen door and take the path we took to get here and then…"

Maggie, stunned at what she heard, asked, "I'm flying us out of here? With what, Greg? Have you forgotten our plane is sitting on a runway in Cuba? Where are you getting this plane?"

"Hand me the water, Maggie. Maybe if I eat this crap and drink a lot of water I won't get sick. To answer your question, we don't have a plane, we have a helicopter. We're using Macedo's chopper to get out of here. And we're doing it in the dead of night. Do you think they can hear the chopper from Macedo's house?" Greg asked.

Maggie put her hand to her forehead and stared at her husband in disbelief. "Damn straight they'll hear that chopper from the house. Are you aware I've ten hours of helicopter instruction and nothing more? You're aware I've never flown a chopper without an instructor sitting next to me.….right?"

Greg smiled, "Yeah, I'm aware of that. I'm also aware you're the best damn pilot in…"

Maggie interrupted, "Don't give me that best pilot bullshit. I cannot fly us outta here. I have six hours of actual flying time. The rest was classroom study. There's more. None of my flying experience was in a Huey. I will not… I cannot fly someone else's helicopter out of this jungle with ten hours of total helicopter training."

Maggie was becoming angry and Greg knew it. She

tried to calm herself enough to explain the realities to Greg. "I haven't had instruction in over a year and a half and that was with a Bell. Besides, Macedo will have the chopper well guarded. So let's see, we have to kill the guards, hope the chopper is of military design and doesn't have an ignition key. I have to figure out how to crank it up, try to take off with a cold engine in the dead of night with no lights and get it off the ground before a small army of guards descends on us and opens fire. Is that about it, baby?"

Greg smiled at his wife, "If anyone can do it, it's you, Maggie."

"Knock off the bullshit, Greg. You ask too much of me. I can't do it!"

Greg frowned at his wife, "Wrong, you mean you won't do it. Here are our options: sit here in the cellar until we are discovered and killed. Steal horses and ride into the jungle as far as we can, then run until we are shot by guards or eaten by an animal. Or we can kill ourselves in a helicopter trying to escape. That third option looks pretty good to me."

"You're too optimistic, Greg. The gunfire from killing the guards watching the helicopter will alert everyone. Then I have to figure out how to start the damn thing and get us off the ground. We have no chance of pulling this off. Please, I beg you, think of another way."

"There's no other way," Greg whispered. "If my memory serves me correctly, it's a twenty minute walk down that path to the chopper. I'm guessing none of the horses are saddled at night so they will have to run the path in darkness to the chopper. We have a full ten minutes to get the hell out of here. I'll help you fly."

"Help me fly? Greg, your total experience with a Huey is rappelling from the bay door. How are you going to help me fly?" Maggie asked.

Greg ignored the question. "Two in the morning is the optimum hour. Everyone, except maybe Macedo, will have given up on finding us. When they find the dead guard in the wine cellar, they'll realize we're armed. Except for Macedo's most loyal men, they'll be reluctant to get themselves killed by rushing down a path to confront a desperate escapee with a Russian automatic weapon. You gotta think like they think. If we're bold and stay positive, this can happen. It will happen. We'll use the element of surprise to kill the guards at the helicopter."

Maggie's mind raced. She closed her eyes and tried to think of her chopper training. She envisioned the helicopter's collective and how it felt in her hand. She reminded herself of the rookie mistakes she had made in her early training that sent her into a violent spin. She mentally lifted the chopper from the grass and held it steady as she rose above the tree line. Continuing her thoughts, she lowered the craft to the landing field. She remembered her instructor complimenting her on her achievements saying she was a natural chopper pilot. Then she remembered the day she quit her training, telling her instructor she was short on money. She promised to start again when money wasn't so scarce. Then Greg got shot and she never went back.

She opened her eyes to look at Greg. Just as she started

to speak, the sound of the cellar door opening caused her to gasp. Blowing out the candle, they slid to a prone position in the back of the cellar as a man walked down the stairs. Light from the kitchen filled the cellar. Greg pulled the AK-47 to his chest and unlocked the safety.

"Shit…a dead rat. I'll find it later," the cook muttered to himself as he flipped on the cellar light, filling the room with light. Still, he couldn't see Greg and Maggie unless he walked toward the back of the cellar. Taking several steps down an aisle, he stopped. Turning on a small penlight to better read the wine labels, he pulled a bottle from its cradle. He was less than eight feet away from Maggie and Greg. Maggie closed her eyes and held her breath while Greg moved his body several inches so he could see through two racks and have visual contact.

The cook turned off his penlight and returned it to his coat pocket. He turned and walked toward the back of the cellar, looking for another bottle of wine.

A voice from the kitchen called out, "Julio, are you down there?"

The cook turned and faced the stairs, "I am. What is it?"

"Macedo is awake. He wants to see you now. Go to his office," the voice called.

The cook turned off the light and climbed the stairs, closing the door behind him.

"My God, that was close. We gotta get outta here. I'd rather be shot on the run than cornered like a rat in this pitch black cellar," Maggie said, waiting for her husband's response.

"You're right, Maggie, if they return to clean up what they think is a dead rat, we'll be discovered. But we'll also not make it in daylight. We must make our move under cover of dark. Let's pray they don't come back until tomorrow morning. I admit I don't have all the details of this plan worked out yet. We'll have to see how it goes tonight. In the meantime, let's sleep as much as we can and be fresh for our move."

Maggie chuckled as she slid forward to be closer to Greg. "Fresh? I smell like a goat and so do you. I'll never be able to sleep knowing I have to fly a chopper I know nothing about. I wish I had as much faith in me as you do."

Greg didn't respond. He put his arm around her and pulled her head to his shoulder. "I love you, Maggie."

CHAPTER FOURTEEN

Greg lit the candle and sat it on the edge of a nearby wine rack. He leaned down and kissed Maggie on the cheek, startling her. "It's time, chopper lady."

Maggie pushed herself up from a prone position and hugged her husband. "If I kill you in the chopper, are you going to be pissed at me?" she joked.

Greg held her, "Of course I'll be mad," he quipped.

As was usually the case, the clowning around was out of nervousness. Maggie knew she probably wouldn't be able to fly Macedo's helicopter but couldn't say no to her husband. Greg knew their chance of even getting to the helicopter and overtaking the guards was next to zero. But both knew they had no good options. Walking into the jungle would be certain death. Killing the guards and flying out seemed less risky, especially since they had no idea where they were or in what direction to walk.

"Listen to me," Greg said to his wife. "We move in short bursts. I'll pick a visible stop point and on my command we'll move low and quick. Once there, I'll pick another stop point and we repeat this until we reach the chopper. If we're intercepted and there's gunfire, we'll run for the chopper and take our chances with whatever awaits us. Do you understand?"

"Sounds like a shitty plan to me," she smiled, knowing they had no other options.

Greg climbed the cellar steps and flipped on the light, lighting up the cellar. Walking back to his hiding spot he shoved the candle and matches into his pocket. They gathered up the rolls and water and placed them in their cargo pockets. Greg checked the status of his weapon, making sure the safety was off.

The two moved toward the cellar door entrance. The stench of the dead guard was overwhelming. Greg climbed the stairs and then reached to turn off the light. Standing in total darkness, they waited on the cellar stairs for their eyes to adjust. After a moment Greg turned the cellar door knob and pushed the door open one inch. Seeing nothing but a dark storage room, he pushed the door open wide but remained motionless. From the cellar entrance, they could hear the noises of the Colombian jungle. The night sky produced enough light for them to get their bearings and locate the outer kitchen door. Pulling his automatic weapon to a firing position, Greg whispered to Maggie. "Okay, we're good to go. Stay glued to me."

Maggie reached out and hooked her finger onto the back of Greg's belt. They entered the kitchen and moved along the wall toward the outer kitchen door. Standing beside the door, they lowered themselves to a crouched position. Greg opened the door. Seeing nothing alarming, the two stood and walked from the kitchen onto a small porch that led to the backyard. They crouched again just outside the door to scan the yard. As Greg reached to pull the door shut, he spotted two people sitting on a yard bench about a hundred feet from the kitchen entrance.

Greg motioned to Maggie, alerting her. The bench was in such a position they wouldn't be able to reach the path without being spotted.

"Damn, it's two fifteen in the morning. What the hell are they doing up?" Greg whispered, not expecting an answer.

Maggie pointed before she spoke, "It's a man and a woman. Maybe lovers, maybe field hands looking at the moon and finding a little romance."

Just then the man leaned over and kissed the woman. They embraced and the kiss was long.

"Right again, Maggie," Greg whispered. "This is great news. Better still, I'm thinking of a better plan than we discussed. But there's no time to talk. You stay here and be ready to move."

Maggie nodded that she understood.

Staying low, Greg moved toward the embraced couple, his weapon at his shoulder, ready to fire. The couple was so occupied with their love-making they were unaware of Greg's approach until he was several feet from them. Seeing him, the woman jumped to her feet and gasped, placing her hand to her mouth.

Thinking it was one of Macedo's guards, the man pleaded in Spanish. "We're sorry to be here but we have no other place to be alone. Please forgive us and please don't tell Master Macedo."

Greg spoke, attempting his best Spanish. "Remain quiet and I won't kill you. If you call out, I'll kill you both. Understand?"

The couple realized they may be in more trouble than they originally thought. It was obvious the man pointing the gun at them was one of the escaped prisoners everyone had been looking for the entire day.

"Please, sir, don't kill us," the male field worker pleaded in Spanish, "We're peasants and don't care about your disagreements with Master Macedo. We'll cooperate. Please don't kill us."

Greg motioned for Maggie to join him. Once she arrived, Greg motioned for the field hands to walk across the yard to the path. Maggie knew this wasn't a good time for questions and asked nothing. The four moved down the slope of the mansion's backyard toward the path. Maggie took the lead with Greg bringing up the rear. Once they had walked fifty yards down the path into the dense jungle, Greg ordered the group to stop.

"Your Spanish is better than mine, Maggie," Greg said. "Tell them we need them to cooperate but if they refuse or alert the guards, they'll be killed. Tell them we're desperate and have nothing to lose."

Without hesitation Maggie repeated the warning to the couple.

Looking at Greg and his weapon, the male field worker spoke, "As I said before, sir, we're not interested in your quarrel with Macedo. We want to live. We'll cooperate."

Before Maggie could translate, Greg put up his hand to stop her. "I understood what he said. Tell him he must walk down this path to where the helicopter is kept. Tell him to announce to the guards he has been sent by Macedo to tell them the prisoners have been captured and killed and they can go to bed. If he doesn't do as we say, we'll kill his woman."

Maggie looked at the field hand. "What's your name?"

"Andre...and this is my girlfriend, Rosa," the field hand said.

As Maggie began to relay the message from Greg, Andre began to shake his head in despair. He appealed to Maggie, placing his hands together as if praying. "If I do that, Master Macedo will have us both killed so we are dead either way. Please let us to return to our homes and we'll say nothing about any of this."

Before Maggie could answer, Greg spoke again, putting his hand on Andre's shoulder. "My Spanish is not so good. I understand. I know you're afraid. You and Rosa will come with us and we'll fly to Guantanamo. There, I'll tell the government you assisted us and you'll get political asylum. I work for the government and have much influence. You can live in America. Do you understand?"

Andre smiled and shook his head, indicating he would cooperate.

Greg was pleased with Andre, but threatened, "Good, we'll take your woman and hide in the jungle where we can observe you if you betray us. Remember, if this doesn't work, Rosa is dead."

Maggie interjected, "Lighten up, Greg, These people are just field hands and..."

Greg interrupted Maggie, ignoring her comment.

"Maggie, tell Andre when we see the guards walk up the path, we'll take his woman…ah, Rosa, to the helicopter. He must find a way to leave the guards and come to the helicopter."

As Maggie repeated the instructions to Andre, he began to nod his head and smile. "The guards will not want to associate with a field hand. They'll expect me to leave them once we clear the path. I'll then run to the helicopter. Please don't leave without me, sir. I'm helping you. If you leave me, they will kill me. Please, promise me."

Greg reached out to shake Andre's hand. "You have my word. We'll wait for you. Now let's get started. Go and tell the guards and good luck."

As Andre disappeared down the path, Greg, Maggie and Rosa crept into the dense jungle and took up a position where they could see anyone passing on the path. Two hours passed and the guards didn't return. Greg grew nervous and felt they may have been betrayed.

Unable to wait any longer, Greg whispered to Maggie. "You take the gun and guard the woman while I check to see what happened."

Maggie shook her head and whispered back, "I know nothing about using this weapon. Is this a good idea, splitting up like this?"

Greg held out the weapon for Maggie to take. "The woman doesn't know that. She'll assume you're proficient with the weapon. The safety is off. Aim and pull the trigger just like the M16. I can't wait here any longer. I'm not going to sit here and be ambushed by the guards."

Maggie nodded and Greg started to make his way

through the dense jungle toward the path. He had not taken more than ten steps when he heard the guards talking. He could tell they were close. Greg dove for cover, trying to conceal himself. He was right at the edge of the path. Fearful he would make too much noise by moving further away, he pulled underbrush over him for concealment. Greg buried his face into the jungle floor and waited motionless as the guards passed by him, almost walking on him.

By now Maggie could hear the guards talking. She pointed her weapon at Rosa and put her finger to her lips. "Shh."

As the guards walked by in single file, Maggie noticed Andre wasn't with them. Not sure what to do, she decided to stay put until Greg returned. Once the guards were well out of sight, Greg returned.

"Okay, let's get the hell out of here," Greg ordered.

"Did you notice Andre wasn't with the guards?" Maggie asked.

"No, I had my face buried," Greg responded. "Maybe he's at the chopper. Or maybe they killed him. You never know about Macedo's guards. They've more respect for their chickens than field hands. Let's hope he's all right."

Once they got near the end of the path, Greg spotted the truck. He pointed, "Look ahead, Maggie, there's the truck, right where the guards left it. Our luck increases by the minute."

The clock was running. If the guards learned they had been duped, they would rush back to the chopper. Greg, Maggie and Rosa climbed quietly into the truck. The keys were in the ignition. Careful not to race the truck's engine,

Greg drove down the road toward the chopper. When they reached the road's end, Macedo's helicopter sat in full view. Sitting in the belly of the chopper with his feet dangling was Andre. He smiled and waved, seeing Rosa was unharmed.

Maggie jumped from the truck and ran to the pilot's seat. Greg detached the three tie-downs holding the chopper in place. While Rosa climbed into the belly of the chopper, Greg took his position as copilot. Maggie stared at the instruments with her hands in her lap. After a moment Greg became nervous.

"Maggie...anytime now. Let's get the hell outta here," Greg said.

"Give me a break, damn it," Maggie snapped back. "I need this time. Doing a vertical ascent and lifting out of this hole in the jungle is the hardest takeoff possible. If you don't want me to crash, then leave me alone. Maybe you should be in the back with Andre and Rosa. If the guards show up, you'll be more helpful in the back than sitting up here breaking my chops."

Greg realized Maggie was right. She was under a tremendous amount of stress and would have one chance to do this right. Without speaking, he grabbed his weapon and slid from his seat, joining Andre and Rosa. He felt helpless sitting in the back, not being able to help Maggie fly the chopper. He was about to jump out of his skin because he knew the guards would return soon. He also had a stomach ache.

Two minutes later, the chopper's engine started and the blades began to slowly turn. Greg looked at his watch and noted they had about fifteen minutes until the guards would arrive.

Maggie leaned back in her seat and called to Greg. "There should be waist straps on the bench seat. Drop the seat and everyone buckle up. This may get rough."

Greg dropped the canvas bench and pointed for the two field hands to sit and buckle themselves in. Then he sat in the middle of the chopper's cargo area with his legs crossed and his weapon in his lap.

As the turbine engine spooled up, so did the main rotor above them until the rpm was at 100% and ready for flight. Maggie was sure the whine of the engine could be heard from the Macedo mansion and knew time wasn't on her side. She grabbed the collective and fingered the cyclic with her other hand. She looked back at Greg.

"Get the hell strapped in, damn it. Are you crazy?" she shouted at her husband.

"I'm no use to you strapped in," he shouted back. "I may have to fire from any angle and I can't do that from the bench. Leave me alone and let me help you."

Maggie focused on her collective control. This was no time for a family dispute. She moved the floor pedals with her feet to feel the pressure needed to move them. It was all beginning to come back to her. She hoped and prayed her ten hours of flight instruction would be enough to save their lives.

Maggie turned to speak with Greg again, possibly for the last time in their lives. "I'm at maximum rotor speed. Hang on to your ass, baby, 'cause here we go."

Greg smiled and gave her a thumbs up as Maggie turned

to face the controls. She fiddled with the collective control, moving it up from a lower stop position, slightly changing the main rotor pitch. The chopper began to get light on its skids. Gaining confidence, Maggie lifted the collective control a bit further and the skid lifted from the grass to a height of one foot. Upon lifting from the ground, the helicopter began to spin out of control completing a quick 360 degree spin before Maggie shoved hard on the left pedal to stabilize the aircraft.

"Shit, shit, shit, I forgot about that," she screamed to herself as the chopper stabilized.

The chopper lifted and maintained an altitude of three feet before it began to wash from side to side. Maggie made corrections with the cyclic control but it was obvious she needed practice. She was consistently overcompensating, making all the rookie mistakes except there was no instructor sitting next to her to save her from a fatal blunder.

She called out to Greg, "I'm turning on the lights so get ready. It doesn't matter anyway and I need to see."

Greg nodded and pulled his automatic weapon to his shoulder pointing it toward the entrance to the path that led to Macedo's mansion. Holding her breath, Maggie fiddled with the collective, causing the aircraft to gain altitude to seven feet. She expelled her air and tried to breathe normal. Wash from the rotor blades against the ground began to sway the aircraft from side to side. Maggie fought to maintain control.

A shot was heard over the whine of the engine and a bullet hole appeared in the roof of the bay area inches from

Greg's head. He could see no one below but fired several rounds toward the path.

Maggie lifted the aircraft to ten feet. Greg spotted two guards run into the clearing and open fire. The windshield on the copilot side of the chopper was riddled with bullet holes and the bullets lodged in the copilot's headrest. Greg leaned forward and opened fire, killing the two guards.

The chopper continued to gain altitude. At one point the rotor blades came close to the dense foliage, clipping several trees and shredding their leaves. Maggie was able to move the aircraft away but she lost altitude. She was so focused on the flight, she hadn't noticed the bullet holes in the windshield. *Patience, Maggie, patience. Slowly lift above the jungle. Focus. Maintain control,* she whispered to herself. As she continued to gain altitude, Greg spotted Macedo riding bareback into the clearing. His horse reared, frightened by the roar of the helicopter.

Macedo held to the reins with one hand and pointed a shotgun with the other. He fired his weapon at the chopper. Greg fell prone to avoid being hit. Two slugs from Macedo's shotgun killed Andre. As he slumped over into Rosa's lap, she screamed in horror.

Greg inched his way to the edge of the chopper's open bay where he could get a better shot. Macedo cranked another round into his weapon and raised his arm to fire again. Greg pulled on his trigger and held it. Bullets sprayed from his weapon. Macedo's horse fell to the ground, pinning Macedo's right leg under the horse. Greg saw he had killed the horse, but not Macedo. He aimed his weapon and filled Macedo's upper torso with bullets. He died instantly.

Maggie was so intent on flying the aircraft she was unaware of what was occurring in the rear of the chopper. They were now several feet above the jungle canopy and most of the ground wash had stopped. The aircraft was stable and Maggie was gaining confidence in keeping it in the air. She tilted the chopper's nose down and increased the collective, causing the chopper to move forward.

As the aircraft distanced itself from the landing sight, Greg could see several of Macedo's guards gathered around Macedo and his horse to look on in disbelief.

"Damn, I'm good. I'm actually flying this frigging thing," Maggie shouted to anyone who could hear. Not getting a response, she turned to see her husband comforting Rosa who was covered with Andre's blood. Her dead boyfriend lay in her lap as she cried, rocking back and forth.

"Oh, God," Maggie muttered under her breath. She called out to Greg over the roar of the wind and chopper engine, "Is he dead?"

Greg nodded and shouted to Maggie, "So is Macedo. Fly the damn chopper. I'll take care of this."

Maggie shouted back, "Ask Rosa where Macedo gets his supplies. Ask her to name the town where they travel for food."

After a moment of conversing with the woman, Greg called back, "Santa Marta. You know where that is?"

"Santa Marta? Damn right I know it. I've flown there. I know the airport director. I bring him toilet paper," Maggie laughed. "It's a coastal town sitting on the edge of the jungle. I'm already heading north so when we reach the coast I'll gain altitude and look for lights. It's a plan, Greg. We are kickin' ass here."

"I disagree," Greg shook his head. "Once you reach the coast, sit this bastard down and we'll take our chances from there. We don't know what damage those bullets did to the chopper."

Maggie nodded in agreement. She couldn't believe their luck. With Macedo dead, she figured no one would be hunting for them and if they found their way to Santa Marta, she could get the airport director to get them back to the States.

In fear of striking a mountainside, Maggie raised the altitude to two thousand feet. The night air grew cool and void of humidity. She was certain they were not far from the coast and was confident she could reach the ocean with a due north heading.

CHAPTER FIFTEEN

"Wake up, Senor Spoto, it's time for breakfast. We brought you black beans and rice. After you've eaten, we'll take you to the showers. We also have fresh clothing for you. You must be alert and ready by 8 AM when we escort you to Commander Castro's private office. Senor Spoto, did you hear any of this?" the prison warden asked.

Pete Spoto lay motionless on his prison cell bed. His mind raced. He hadn't missed a word and knew the odds of him living in a prison for the rest of his life had somehow diminished. A prison guard poked his leg with a baton.

"Senor Spoto, time to get going. Wake up."

Pete sat up in his bed. His eye was still swollen and his vision still blurred from the beating. He cleared his throat before taking the plate of food from the guard and, sitting it on his lap, he asked, "Why am I going to see Raul?"

"Please, Mr. Spoto, show some respect. Refer to him as Commander Castro or Commodore Castro," the warden admonished him. "We would show your President Nixon the same respect."

Pete ignored the reprimand and ate his food. He couldn't remember ever being so hungry and the rice and bean meal was delicious. He held up his fork and smiled, "My compliments to the chef. Are these Russian beans?"

The warden turned to leave. "I'll leave you now but will be waiting for you at the gate for your trip to see the commander. My guards will see to your needs."

"Wait, Mr. Warden, do you have wine to help me wash this down?" Pete asked.

The warden ignored the request and disappeared down the dim hallway.

After being taken to the showers, Pete put on a pair of beige cotton pants and a white Guayabera shirt that fit him perfectly as did the sandals. While he was excited about what might be occurring, he also realized that Raul Castro may be setting him up to kill him. It was his way. He loved to kill his prisoners when they least expected it. Pete put the thought of his death aside since there was nothing he could do about it anyway. Most of all, he hated not being in control of his destiny.

Two guards escorted Pete to the front gate of Havana's prison. A 1955 Cadillac waited in front of the prison. As Pete and the guards approached, the driver opened a rear door and the three got in. Pete sat in the middle with a guard on each side. The prison warden sat motionless in the front passenger seat.

The twenty-seven mile ride from the prison to downtown Havana was uneventful. It had been three years since Pete had been to Havana. He had been on an undercover assignment to hook up with three Colombian smugglers for the purpose of coordinating the movement and transfer of thousands of pounds of marijuana into Miami.

As the Cadillac grew closer to Havana, Pete spoke. "Not much has changed. The place still looks like shit."

No one responded. The car pulled up to the front gates of the Palace of the Revolution, the driver turned off the engine and everyone sat motionless.

After five minutes, Pete grew uncomfortable and asked, "Excuse me but does the air work in this car. It's hot as hell back here. You don't want me to be all sweaty when I meet Commander Castro now, do you?" Pete joked.

Ten minutes later, the gates were opened and the Cadillac pulled up to a side building immediately to the left of the main entrance. Out walked Raul, smiling and waving at Pete.

He stuck his hand through the Cadillac's open window, reached across a guard and shook Pete's hand. "Comrade, we meet once again. Please, come with me to my office."

Pete muttered under his breath, "What a bunch of bullshit. What's going on?"

The prison guards opened both back doors of the car and Pete got out on the side where his new friend, Raul, stood. He was escorted into the building by military soldiers in clean pressed dress uniforms. The four walked straight to Raul's office where Pete was offered a seat on a couch away from the desk. Castro sat next to him. The two armed guards were joined by two more guards who stood near the two doors at opposite ends of the office.

"So, Commander Castro, what's on your mind? You didn't get me all cleaned up and fed just so we could have a

196

social visit. What's going on? Are we no longer enemies?" Pete asked.

Castro smiled and gestured toward a liquor cabinet before speaking. "May I offer you a Russian vodka? The best filtered vodka in the world. To mix this with anything would be a crime. It is best sipped slowly. May I pour?" Castro asked.

"I don't drink the hard stuff anymore. A little wine with dinner and that's about it for me. Why am I here?"

"I'll get right to the point," Raul spoke. "Your friends have escaped and can't be found. Pedro Macedo has been killed by Captain Strong and now I have a need to strike another business deal that can be advantageous to us both."

Pete looked at Castro in disbelief. He wanted to laugh but knew better. Macedo and Castro were good friends and Pete assumed Castro was in a bad mood. After a moment of hesitation, Spoto pointed to his swollen eye and said, "You gotta be shittin' me. Another business deal? I never had a deal with you. My agreement was with Macedo. All you ever did was put me in prison and beat the shit out me. Now you want my help?"

"It's complicated," Castro said as he pulled a cigar from his top pocket. "Macedo deceived you, not me. After your agreement with him, he contacted me because he knew of my hatred for you. As a favor to me, he offered you as a gift, a gift I couldn't refuse. But now things have changed. I need Strong dead more than I need you rotting in my prison. Everyone must pay for their crimes while on earth. If I'm lucky, you'll kill each other."

"You want me to kill Strong?" Pete asked. "I can't pull the trigger on him. You ask too much."

"You're full of shit, Senor Spoto," Raul snapped back. "You already arranged his death once and now you say you can't kill him?" Raul laughed, rising from the couch. He looked down on the bruised and beaten man while waiting for a reply.

"Arranging a meeting is different than pulling the trigger on an old friend...ex old friend. I know you find it hard to distinguish the difference, but there's a difference," Pete responded.

"You have strange morals, Mr. Spoto. So do I send you back to rot in my prison or do I set you free?"

Pete didn't answer. He sat pondering what he had been told. *How did Greg and Maggie escape from a fortress in the middle of a Colombian jungle? Was this another Cuban lie and, if so, why? There's something missing here. Cuba doesn't need me to kill Strong. What the hell are they up to?* Pete wondered.

"You have operatives working in Miami. Why not have them kill Strong?" Pete asked.

Castro lit his cigar before speaking, "Because I take delight in you killing him. I predict you'll head straight to the Strong house where you know $400,000 is hidden somewhere. That, coupled with whatever you did with your payment, means you'll be living pretty well."

"How do you know I won't split? It's a big world and I could disappear and live pretty damn well with the money I have," Pete suggested.

Castro took a drag from his cigar, "Are you the dumbest

DEA agent in America? Are you trying to talk me out of this? You want me to throw you back in my prison? What the hell are you thinking?"

Pete was wondering the same thing. He tried to smile but it hurt so badly, he just grinned before speaking. "Because I don't understand any of this and I hate operating not knowing where I stand. I need to get more comfortable with this plan. I need more."

"All right, Mr. Spoto, I'll give you more. I know you're an opportunist and will do this for the money and your freedom. You won't split because you've a daughter working for Financial Federal Bank on Miami Beach. You'll be concerned about the welfare of her and her two children. That's the same bank where you have the government deposit your pension check," Castro said. "If you love your daughter as much as I think you do, you'll find Greg Strong, shoot him in the head and live on that money and your pension."

Pete stood up to face Castro. They stared at each other. Castro had a smirk on his face as he took another drag from his cigar.

Pete spoke, "You don't happen to have another one of those cigars, do you?"

Castro laughed, reaching for another cigar. "We'll provide you with one thousand American dollars and transportation to America. Since you left your passport in the plane, we have it. We would prefer to fly you to Mexico City. I'll arrange for you to be smuggled into Texas. I'll just hang on to your passport until you've completed your mission."

Castro reached to light Spoto's cigar. Pete grabbed the lighter from him and lit his cigar. Blowing smoke toward

Castro, Pete said, "We have a deal. I'll do as you ask. I'll need time to recover from my beating and I have to find Strong. Don't put tight time restraints on me."

Castro reached out his hand. "Goodbye, Mr. Spoto. Let's hope we don't ever meet again. If we do, it will be because you have betrayed me."

As the two guards escorted Spoto from the office, he turned to speak, "Tell the warden to put less salt in the beans."

Castro's grin grew wide. "I will. And, oh, Senor Spoto, I don't want you to leave thinking I bought that bullshit story about you not working for President Nixon. We happen to know you are, as a matter of fact, working for him but it doesn't matter. Just take care of your assignment. Good day, Pete Spoto."

CHAPTER SIXTEEN

Maggie continued to struggle with Macedo's helicopter. Light, gusty winds were playing havoc with her ability to fly and hold a northerly course. Because of the wind, she continuously overcompensated with her corrections, causing her aircraft to gain and lose altitude. They had flown less than fifty miles and she had almost crashed twice. Her stress level was to a maximum. She had thrown up in her lap, a combination of bad water and nerves. She knew as they got closer to the ocean the sudden gusts of air would grow stronger. She questioned her ability to land.

Maggie turned in her seat to speak to Greg, "I didn't sign up for this, ya know," she shouted over the roar of the engine. "This wasn't what we discussed as part of the plan. I should be home in bed by now but instead I'm about to crash land this damn chopper."

Greg knew she was talking to him but couldn't hear what she said because he was engrossed in conversation with Rosa who was still holding her dead boyfriend's head in her lap. Her sobbing had subsided.

"Rosa...please listen to me," Greg spoke, using his limited Spanish. "Andre has gone to heaven. We must push his remains out or there'll be trouble and you won't go to America. Maybe you'll go to a Colombian jail. All of us may go to jail," Greg gestured to her with his arms. "Do you understand me, Rosa?"

Rosa stared into Greg's eyes, not wanting to agree with him but knew he was right. She nodded and turned her head away so she wouldn't have to watch. Greg dragged Andre's body from the bench and onto the belly of the chopper. Putting Andre's arms over his head made it easy to roll his body to the edge of the bay door. With a hard push, Andre disappeared into the night.

Greg sat back on the bench and put both arms around Rosa. "You must tell no one about this, do you understand?"

She started to cry again, then pushed herself away from Greg and nodded.

"Good! You'll have a good life in America. You'll see," Greg said, trying to bolster her spirits. "Now you stay here and I'll be back soon."

Greg crawled to the front of the chopper and leaned between the seats, noticing the vomit in her lap. "How's it goin, babe? What can I do to help?"

Maggie reached out and removed the spare headset hanging from a small hook on the co-pilot's side of the chopper and held it out. "Put this on so we can talk," she ordered. "We're doing seventy knots. I'm afraid to go any faster. I'm having trouble keeping this sucker stable. I keep overcompensating when we're hit with a gust of wind. My nerves are shot. I want to warn you, Greg, we're not out of this by a long shot. I may still kill us in a crash landing."

Greg pulled the microphone stem closer to his lips. "That's exactly what I want you to do, Maggie. I want a controlled crash landing. Are you up for that?"

"You're insane, Greg! Are you saying you want me to crash this helicopter?"

Maggie wanted to look at her husband, but had to keep her eyes on flying. She took a quick look to see if he was still right behind her. "Well, are ya going to tell me, or what? Why are we killing ourselves in a crash?"

Greg put his hand on Maggie's shoulder. "We're not killing ourselves. We're saving our asses. The chopper is covered with Andre's blood. So is Rosa's dress, hands, arms and face. It looks like she took a bath in her boyfriend's blood. There's blood all over the bench, in every crevice of the bench, in the bench hinges, between the floor plates under the bench and a hundred other places."

"So what are you suggesting we do? Create a fiery crash and hope we don't burn to death?" Maggie asked, knowing it must be the wrong answer.

"You're going to land in deep water. Once the water stops the rotation of the blades, we'll swim to safety. Can you sit this thing down gently in the ocean, Maggie?" Greg asked.

Maggie smiled, "I don't know about gently, but I can get us over water and kill the engine. The chopper will fall slowly and the tip of the blades will strike the water and stop them long before the cockpit is submerged. Hopefully a rotor blade won't break off and decapitate me. I'll have to crash with my door open. Once I feel the ocean on my body, I'll unbuckle and swim to land. I can do it, Greg, even in the dark."

"Okay then, it's a plan. By the time Colombian authorities find it and fish it out of the ocean, there'll be no semblance of blood on us or the aircraft. Everyone and everything gets a bath. Hmmm, I wonder if Rosa can swim."

"Greg, don't tell her about this. If she doesn't swim, she may panic when she hears the plan. We'll deal with her in the water," Maggie proposed.

"I agree, Maggie. I'll look for vests. You look under your seat."

Maggie reached under her seat. "It's empty. Check the overhead bins."

Maggie flew the helicopter northward at two thousand feet elevation, maintaining her altitude the best she could. She scanned the horizon for the lights of Santa Marta. She knew if she kept a due north heading, they would have to see water soon. Maggie leaned forward to adjust an instrument and Greg noticed the back of her black, long sleeved shirt was soaking wet with perspiration.

"Bad news, Maggie, the bins are empty. Don't these people believe in safety? We'll have to swim without vests. Let's just hope there's no rip tide. Remember to swim with the coast line if the tide keeps us from shore. Just before you put us in the water, I'll ask Rosa if she swims."

Maggie nodded but wouldn't take her eyes from her instrument panel and the night sky in front of her.

Greg sat on the floor just behind the co-pilot's seat. The moon produced enough light for him to see her profile. He stared at her, remembering how much he loved her. He pulled himself up and kissed her cheek.

"Stop that, Greg." Maggie ordered. "You want me to lose control of this damn thing? Besides I know I smell like puke."

"All right, I'll leave you alone. I'm taking off the headset and I'm going to sit with Rosa."

Maggie managed to keep her aircraft steady for the next hour. After passing over a mountain peak, she spotted the twinkle of lights on the ground. She knew it could be Santa Marta and relief poured over her.

She called out to Greg, "I've got civilization. I've got lights, maybe forty miles off our starboard."

Greg reached for a handhold near the open chopper door and leaned forward. "I see it, Maggie. Let's crash about ten miles southwest of the town. Kill your lights and I think we should start descending. What do you think?"

"I'm already starting descent to one thousand and nudging more east. I'm actually going to pull this off. I don't believe it!"

"I had confidence in you, Maggie. You're one hell of a pilot. And pretty, too," Greg joked.

Greg looked at Rosa and pointed toward the lights. She faked a smile and nodded. He knew she was still the weak link in their escape. If taken into custody, she may break down and tell her story to the Colombian police. On the other hand, Greg hoped they could avoid the police by convincing Maggie's friend at the airport to help them escape.

Maggie turned her head and shouted, "Okay, that's Santa Marta. I can see the airport beacon. They should have us on radar by now, that is, if anyone is awake. I'm dropping to three hundred feet. I can see the ocean. It's time to tell Rosa we are going to get wet."

Greg crawled back to the bench seat where Rosa was buckled.

"Rosa, can you swim?" Greg asked, moving his arms in a swimming motion.

She stared at him, speechless at first. Then she mustered a smile and nodded.

"Good, Rosa, we're going to land in the ocean," Greg told her.

As the dim glow of Santa Marta grew brighter, the aircraft continued to descend and the ocean grew closer. Maggie leveled the aircraft to one hundred feet and maintained altitude. She was surprised at the calmness of the air as the aircraft drew closer to the water. She had expected more turbulence.

Suddenly the ocean was right underneath them and the decision as to where to crash was at hand.

"Greg, I need you up here," Maggie called out.

Greg looked at Rosa, "It's time to swim, Rosa. You must be brave."

Not waiting for her response, Greg crawled to the front of the chopper and leaned between the seats.

The moon was just starting to vanish and soon the night sky would be darker. Fortunately, this would be to their advantage as they could use the darkness to better hide. The sun wouldn't be up for another hour.

Maggie banked her aircraft, making a wide arc over

the water. "Where da ya want me to dump this thing?" she
asked.

"Well, I'm not sure," Greg responded. "The water looks
calm from here but you never know about the tide. I want
us out far enough that we are in deep water but not out so
far we can't make it to shore if there's a rip tide. You got any
ideas?"

"That makes a big difference. How about Rosa? Does
she swim?"

"Yes, Rosa swims but I don't know whether she is as
strong a swimmer as us. I'll help her if she struggles. How
about if we put down about three hundred feet off shore? Can
we swim a football field?" Greg asked.

"I can if my life depends on it," Maggie said. "Okay,
we're going in. Get buckled."

Greg returned to the canvas bench and strapped himself
in. He instructed Rosa to keep her hand on the buckle release
and the moment she felt water on her body to release herself
from the seat.

Maggie dropped to twenty feet, switched on the landing
lights and banked the chopper toward the shore. When she
felt she was a hundred yards off shore, she attempted to
stabilize the aircraft into a hover. The chopper began to wash
back and forth and spin. It lowered into the ocean. Once the
skids submerged, the chopper sank fast and leaned to the left.
A blade hit the water and broke off. It went flying upwards
and out of her sight. The collision slowed the rotation to a
point that the remaining blade survived the impact with the
water. The chopper rolled over and began to sink.

In a flash, Greg and Rosa were unbuckled and out the

bay door as water rushed in. Maggie unbuckled herself and realized she still had her headset on. She pulled it from her head and flung it toward the copilot's seat as water swirled in around her chest. She rolled out of her seat and into the ocean.

In an instant, the aircraft disappeared from sight. The three survivors began to dog paddle toward shore. Greg cradled his weapon on his upper arms as he paddled. The tide wouldn't be a problem as it had just crested. In a short time, the three were standing on the beach, looking out to sea.

"We are blessed, Greg," Maggie said. "A few hours ago we were awaiting our death in Macedo's storeroom. Since then we've found a way out and have been able to, with the grace of God's help, fly away from our prison and be standing on this beach. And you killed Macedo which should make the Nixon people happy."

"You're not getting religious on me, are ya, Maggie?"

"Yeah, I guess I am, Greg. How else could we have pulled this off? Bill and Duke are dead and we should be also. And who knows about Pete? I'm sure he's dead, too. But we're here and probably going to make it."

"I've one question for you, Maggie," Greg responded. "Are you aware that when you're super stressed you always say 'Shit, shit, shit?' Are you conscious of that?"

Maggie reached to hug her husband. She whispered in his ear, "I know. I can't help myself. I did that all the way through flight school. Be nice, it's my only vice."

CHAPTER SEVENTEEN

Far out at sea, a distant thunderstorm lit the dawn sky, creating a spectacular display of lightening bolts arching from cloud to cloud, some of them striking the ocean. Greg, Maggie and Rosa sat huddled close to each other on the beach. Drained of energy, they quietly watched the performance. It was a typical Colombian dawn, a constant threat of rain and high humidity. Temperatures would reach the nineties by mid-afternoon.

Rosa hugged Maggie's arm and held it tightly.

"You're going to be fine," Maggie assured her. "My husband will find a way to get you to America. We won't leave you in Colombia."

Rosa lifted her head and released her grip on Maggie's arm. "I've been a field worker my whole life. I haven't traveled very far from where I was born and I cannot read or write well. But I know this much. In Colombia, you can trust no one. Do you know that?" Rosa asked.

"We know. But my husband is very smart and I know the manager of the airport in Santa Marta. We'll find a way," Maggie assured Rosa, holding both her hands and squeezing them.

Greg stood up, brushing sand from his wet pants. "Don't make promises you can't keep. Rosa is right, Maggie. How much can we trust your friend at the airport? For all you know, he could be an ally of Macedo."

Before speaking, Maggie stood to be at eye level with her husband. "I don't think so. The guy is always asking me to bring him stuff from the states, like toilet paper and tooth paste. I know he has a wife and a bunch of kids. He doesn't fit the profile of a cartel smuggler. My guess is he just looks the other way to avoid being killed. But I realize speaking to him puts us at risk. Got a better idea?"

"Actually I don't," Greg responded. "But understand this. Fidel Castro has a close loyal friend named Losada whose nickname is 'Red Beard.' He's connected with the M-19 Colombian guerrillas. Cuba's ambassador to Colombia is a guy named Ravelo who is asshole buddies with Losada. M-19 raises money by smuggling dope out of the country and Ravelo greases the skids. Furthermore, if Losada…"

"Hold it, baby. What does that have to do with us getting out of this hellhole? Just bottom line me, will ya?" Maggie asked.

"I'm asking you to connect the dots, Maggie. Ravelo is helping the guerrillas get dope out of Colombia. Everyone is corrupt and getting a piece of the action. The bottom line is that if the Santa Marta airport is being used to transport dope to Cuba, then we can't trust your friend."

Discouraged, Maggie sat back down in the sand. "Damn,

I wish Pete were here. He would find a way for us to get out. What have they done with him, Greg?"

Greg sat next to his wife. "I'm guessin' he's still in Cuba. It doesn't matter. Castro's brother hates him just as much as Macedo does. My guess is he's dead."

The sun had begun to creep above the horizon and the thunderstorm at sea had run its course. Small land crabs inched from their holes, curious to see humans near their homes. Rosa stared at her two new friends and knew, even though she couldn't understand one word of English, they were worried.

"Are we still in trouble?" she asked.

Maggie ignored her question and turned to Greg. "Again, this is my decision. This time I have the plan. The manager at the airport is my friend so this is my call. His name is Manuel and he's a gentleman. I'm bettin' he can be trusted. Just in case, you and Rosa will stay put and I'll walk to Santa Marta and find him. No sense all of us getting killed."

Greg jumped to his feet and protested, "Not on your life am I letting you walk to Santa Marta alone. Look at how you're dressed. The police will be at the airport and when they see an American woman dressed in black, you'll be stopped and questioned. Forget it. You're not going. That's final."

"Relax, for crying out loud," Maggie assured Greg. "You're not giving me much credit here. Listen to my plan. I'll change clothes with Rosa. My blond hair will not be a problem because many Colombian women have bleached their hair blond. I'll walk the ten or so miles to Santa Marta and head to the airport. I know how to get there and then..."

"Bullshit, Maggie," Greg interrupted. "I'll never see you again. I won't allow this."

"Will you shut up for a minute?" Maggie said, losing her temper. "When I bring Manuel supplies from the states, he always has me taxi to a small isolated hangar on the far south side of the airfield. He pulls his car into a hangar and we unload his supplies into his car. He doesn't want his employees or anyone else for that matter to see he's getting goods from America. Now comes the…"

"Maggie, I love you," Greg interrupted again. "Remember what Macedo said he was going to do to you before he killed you. Isn't that burned into your memory? No, Maggie, if we're to die, we'll die together. I'm not letting you go alone."

"Sometimes, Greg, you're the biggest pain in my ass," Maggie scolded him. "Who are you going to change clothes with? Do you really think you can walk around Santa Marta dressed like a damn commando and not get stopped? I'm begging you to use common sense here, Greg. You keep interrupting me before I can finish. Can you just not interrupt me, damn it?"

Rosa jumped to her feet and held Maggie. "I don't understand what is happening but I'm afraid that your fight is not good. Please don't fight."

Greg turned to face the ocean. He knew Maggie was right but couldn't bring himself to allow her to be placed in such grave danger. He felt out of control. Waiting on the beach with Rosa while Maggie attempted to meet with her friend was impossible for him to grasp. He kept thinking if it wasn't for him and his burning desire to kill Harkin, she wouldn't be in this position. Guilt and despair set in and he struggled to think of another plan that wouldn't place Maggie in such danger.

"I'm sorry, Maggie. Tell me the rest of your plan," Greg whispered.

"Good! Thank you. I know this airport well. The hangar where I meet Manuel sits next to the fence that surrounds the airport grounds. It's located at the most isolated part of the town and the chain link fence surrounding the airport is only six feet high and no barbed wire. I'll walk to the south side of the airport, jump the fence and use the wall phone in the hangar to reach the airport switchboard and get connected to Manuel. If he's not in his office, the switchboard will know how to find him. Once, when he didn't show up at the hangar for his supplies, I used that phone and found him. I know I can do this."

Greg shoved his hands into his pants' pockets and stared at his wife. Maggie could see the tension in his face. It was killing him to admit she was right but there was no other feasible way for them to get out of Colombia. Rosa was right. No one could be trusted but if he had to pick a person, it would be Maggie's friend.

"Offer him twenty thousand dollars for his help," Greg said as he held out his arms to hold his wife. "Do you know how many Colombian pesos equals twenty thousand dollars? Even if your friend, Manuel, is in with the cartel people, he might be willing to do this so he can make the money. He'll have to know you can't pay him until you get to America. There must be trust. You're…"

"Greg, I can do this," Maggie interrupted. "How will I find you and Rosa when I return?"

Greg scanned the beach. "See that rotted, washed up log over there? I'll drag it away from the tide line and out on the sand, dig a shallow hole and push one end of the log upright into the hole. You won't be able to miss it. We'll find a place nearby where we can see the marker but be out of sight. When you return, look for this marker."

Maggie was already explaining the plan to Rosa. Without hesitation Rosa began to disrobe and in a matter of minutes Maggie was wearing the clothes of a field hand. Maggie twirled her hair to the top of her head and fastened it in place.

Greg hugged his wife. "It's amazing how different you look, Maggie. Good luck and know I'll be praying that you pull this off. If you don't, then know how much I love you and how sorry I am I got you into this mess. I'm going to…"

"Hush, Greg," Maggie interrupted once again. "You've said enough. I appreciate the prayers but this is going to work. I'm going to make it work. Bye, baby! I love you."

Without hesitation, Maggie headed east down the coastline, into the sun and toward Santa Marta. Greg and Rosa stood on the beach watching Maggie walk away until she eventually disappeared around a slight bend of the beachhead.

"Okay, Rosa, let's find a place to hide until Maggie returns."

Rosa nodded and the two walked off the beach and into the scrub palms and palmetto bushes. One hundred feet off the sandy beach, they found a large fallen tree trunk. Sitting behind the tree, they couldn't be seen from the beach.

***

It was a long day for Greg and Rosa. Doing nothing wasn't something Greg did well. Worry overcame him. The sun was low in the sky and Maggie had not returned. Twice, Greg walked from their hiding spot out to the beach to look for Maggie. Once he saw a figure far in the distance but it turned out to be a fisherman.

The sun set and darkness filled the sky.

"Oh, Mister Greg, I'm afraid for Maggie," Rosa told Greg, speaking in slow, deliberate Spanish.

Greg reached out and held her. "I know, Rosa, I'm also afraid but we'll find a way, even if Maggie doesn't return."

***

Greg sat staring at Rosa, wearing Maggie's black pants and utility shirt. She had fallen asleep, using her folded arm for a pillow. A distant storm far at sea was just beginning its evening performance. He held up his watch to catch the moonlight. *Oh, God, this is turning to shit,* he thought as he saw it was approaching 1 AM. *Here I am, stranded in a hostile country with no passport and with a field worker who speaks no English. Pete and Bill are dead and Maggie is probably also dead. I'm at a loss what to do,* Greg pondered.

At first Greg wasn't sure but thought he heard a car engine so he lifted himself to a kneeling position to scan the beach. He saw nothing. After a minute he was certain a car was coming in his direction. He dropped to a prone position and woke Rosa. She woke with a start and Greg put his hand over her mouth and put his finger to his lips. She nodded. The sound of the car got louder. From their

215

prone position, neither Greg nor Rosa could see the beach. They waited.

The vehicle drove directly to the marker post Greg had planted in the sand and the car's engine stopped. *They've either tortured Maggie into giving up our position or it was her coming for us*, Greg thought as he heard the two car doors slam.

Nothing happened. There was dead silence. Then he heard Maggie's voice. "Come out, come out, wherever you are," she joked. Greg and Rosa jumped to their feet and saw Maggie and a man standing ten feet from a Toyota Land Cruiser.

Cautiously, Greg and Rosa walked toward the beach. When Maggie spotted them walking toward her, she called out, opening her arms wide. "How do ya like me now, baby?"

Greg ran to greet her. He kissed her passionately and held her so tight it cut off her breathing. Maggie tried to push away. "Hey, can I breathe already?"

"Damn, I was worried about you," Greg scolded her, now realizing she was safe. "Where the hell have you been?"

Greg chuckled to himself, realizing how funny that sounded, remembering that was what Maggie usually said to him after not returning from work on time.

"Greg, this is my good friend, Manuel, who speaks English well. Manuel, this is my pain-in-the-ass husband, Greg, and this lady is our good friend, Rosa," Maggie said, making the formal introductions.

Manuel reached out to shake Greg's hand but ignored Rosa.

"You never cease to amaze me, Maggie, but again, where have you been?" Greg asked.

"Okay, let me explain," Maggie responded. "The plan went perfect. I jumped the fence undetected and Manuel was in his office. He drove out to the hangar to meet me. He's willing to help us for thirty thousand American dollars, not twenty. He also insisted we wait until after midnight to make our move. There was no way for me to tell you so I just hoped you would stay put."

"Thank you, Manuel," Greg smiled holding out his hand again to shake Manuel's hand. "You can trust we'll get the money to you as soon as we get home."

Manuel smiled and reached to touch Greg's shoulder. "I trust Maggie and that's why I'm standing here. Bad news travels fast in Colombia and I already knew Macedo had been killed. You are wanted by both the government and the guerrillas. You must know Maggie can never return to Santa Marta."

"The guerrillas might pay you a lot more than thirty thousand for our heads. Did you consider that?" Greg asked, still wondering whether he could trust Manuel.

"Macedo sometimes used my airport to smuggle dope to Cuba and I knew it. Macedo also knew I was uncooperative and would call the police if I found cocaine in my airport. I wasn't on his payroll but I'll admit I didn't pursue him," Manuel said proudly.

"I understand. That's perfectly understandable. Tell me, can you help us?" Greg asked.

"Come and sit in my truck and I'll give you the details as we drive back to Santa Marta," Manuel said as he walked back to his vehicle. "You like my Land Cruiser? It's brand new and I haven't found terrain around Santa Marta this truck cannot conquer."

Greg looked to Maggie for any signal she may want to give to alert him this might be a setup. Maggie picked up on the look and grabbed Greg's arm before speaking. "This is on the up and up, baby. The extra ten grand is for the pilot who will take us to Matamoras, Mexico, on the Texas border. That same pilot will then smuggle us by Jeep into Texas before dawn. I'm confident we're not being ambushed. Trust me."

CHAPTER EIGHTEEN

TWO WEEKS LATER

Maggie stepped from her shower and wrapped a small towel around her hair. The bathroom was filled with steam, making visibility poor. She reached for her bath towel and covered her upper torso. Walking to the small bathroom window, she opened the blinds.

The snow had increased and the wind blew toward the window causing it to pile up on the sill. She stared at the wintry scene and allowed her mind to wander.

Since escaping from Colombia, she couldn't take her mind off the death and misery she and Greg created by agreeing to Pete's proposal. Duke, who wanted to do nothing more than be a good dog, was gone from their lives forever. She remembered when Riley's wife heard her husband had been murdered, she shook her head and muttered something under her breath before walking away. *Riley was an illiterate jerk but he didn't deserve to die the way he did,* she thought as she began drying her lower body. Then she remembered poor

Andre, the field hand, a man whose only crime was being at the wrong place at the wrong time.

And then there was Pete. What happened to him remained a mystery. The logical part of her brain insisted he was dead but there was a side that said he wasn't. Last night, while lying in bed next to Greg she told him she couldn't put Pete to rest unless she saw him being lowered into the ground. Greg reminded her they thought they had done that once already.

Maggie walked to the large mirror on the opposite side of her bathroom. Pulling the small towel from her head, she wiped the steam from the mirror, revealing her new coal black "Kim Novak" haircut. Leaning over the sink, she rubbed the towel through her hair to dry it and remove any remaining loose hairs from the morning haircut and dye job.

Unless the storm worsened, Greg would drive her to the Atlanta airport where her Twin Beech was being stored. She would meet with a fellow pilot, Gaby, who allowed Maggie to share her hangar. Gaby, an old trusted friend of the Strongs, had agreed to deliver the thirty grand they owed Manuel since she flew to Santa Marta regularly. Maggie thought about the government's Twin Beech and how it was probably still sitting on the cartel's landing strip in Cuba. She guessed they would strip it of its engines and anything else of value before setting it on fire.

Weather permitting, Maggie would fly her plane back to Toccoa and try to get her life back to normal. With Harkin and Macedo dead, both she and Greg had experienced enough adventure for a while.

Halderman had not tried to reach them so they decided

to call him. After three attempts, leaving messages each time, they gave up. Halderman never returned their calls. They were not surprised. Each day, it seemed as if President Nixon was getting himself deeper and deeper connected to a break-in at the Watergate complex and they guessed that was at least part of the reason why Halderman had not returned their calls.

Maggie finished drying herself, put on a robe and took a last look at her new haircut that Greg described as "foxy." She walked into the bedroom and was surprised to see Greg sitting on the bed.

"You're back already? Did you get what you needed from the hardware store?" Maggie asked as she dropped her robe and started to dress.

"I did...and guess who I bumped into?" Greg asked.

"I give up, who?"

"Officer Hudson."

"Oh yeah, did Emery's wife have her baby yet and was it a boy or a girl?"

Pulling a sweatshirt over her head, she looked in the bedroom mirror and ruffed up her new haircut and asked, "You really think I'm foxy?"

"Sit next to me on the bed and let's talk" Greg responded, ignoring her question. "Yes, Officer Hudson is the proud father of a seven pound baby boy, born three days ago. His wife is doing fine."

Greg paused, looking down. Maggie put her hand on his upper leg and asked, "Wanna mess around? I just showered."

He ignored the invitation. "Officer Hudson also told me

he saw the guy who was at our house back when we reported an intruder in our driveway. He was sure it was him but didn't say hello because he couldn't remember his name. He asked if he was our house guest."

"Spoto? Pete Spoto? Are you kidding, babe? You're joking, right?" Maggie asked.

"No, Maggie, I'm not kidding," Greg said solemnly "This is serious and I'm deeply concerned. According to Hudson, Pete was seen two days ago but we haven't seen hide nor hair of him. Where the hell is he? Why hasn't he come by the house. Why hasn't he called? What the hell's going on, Maggie? This stinks."

"I agree, Greg. You know I never trusted the guy. He's so damn spooky. What do you think is going on?" Maggie asked.

Greg hesitated, staring into Maggie's eyes. "Did I ever tell you that you have beautiful eyes?"

"Yes, a thousand times," Maggie answered, growing impatient. "I'm becoming frightened all over again, damn it. God, will this ever be over? Tell me what you think, Greg."

Greg rose from his bed and opened his nightstand, pulling out his service revolver from under a towel. "I think there's a reason for concern. Pete is either here for a friendly visit or he's here on a mission. My guess is he's not here to visit because why would he be in town for two days and not call or come by? If Pete has deceived us, it would explain how Macedo and his henchmen knew so much about us."

Shoving the revolver into his pants, Greg sat back on the bed next to Maggie. "There are things…details about the Harkin kidnapping and our eventual capture that keep swimming around in my head. For instance, how did common Cuban soldiers know we were married? And how did the lead soldier know my nickname was The Predator? And why was Pete separated from the team and left in Cuba? How did the Phantom pilot know exactly where we were the night of our capture? No, Maggie, there's much room for concern."

"I'm confused," Maggie responded. "Why would Pete wait in Cypress when all he would have to do is drive out to our house and, after hugs and handshakes, shoot us both? This doesn't make sense."

"Well, I'm guessin' he screwed up and was spotted by Hudson. He wouldn't call the house and hang up because he knows that puts me on alert. He needs the element of surprise." Greg paused as his head filled with ideas. "He was trying to find out if we had returned to the house before making his move but he was spotted by Hudson first. My guess is he's left town and will wait for a better, more opportune time to make his move."

"Wait, Greg. Are we making ourselves crazy here? This is your best friend we're talking about. This is Pete Spoto we're talking about. Are we losing it?" Maggie asked.

"I know...and maybe we are. I'm just not sure. One thing for certain, if Pete is out gunning for me...us, he'll use the element of surprise and we won't have a chance. Remember, I know how he works."

Maggie put her hand to her mouth. "You said us. Do you think he'll want to kill us both?"

Greg reached over to hug his wife. "Maggie, my guess is he doesn't want to kill either of us but has gotten himself in some kind of situation where he has no choice. Who knows for certain?"

"Oh God, the thought of having Pete out to kill us sends more than just chills down my spine. I may never sleep again, you know that, don't you?" Maggie said. "I guess you're tired of me asking, but have you thought of a plan?"

"I have," Greg responded. "I'll drive you to Atlanta and drop you off at Gaby's place. You stay with her for a few days and when I've found the truth about Pete's visit to Cypress, I'll call you. When it's safe, you can fly back to Toccoa and I'll pick you up."

Maggie got up from the bed and walked to her end table, opened a lower drawer and removed her small five shot revolver. She held the gun up in plain view, making sure Greg could see it. "I don't like your plan even a little bit. We're a team, right? I'm the person watching your back, right? Or did you forget? I'm Maggie Strong, wife of Captain Greg Strong, the infamous predator and the strongest man on the force who shoots the wings off of flies from a hundred yards. Where you go, I go, and that's final."

"Put the damn gun away, Maggie," Greg ordered. "We're not even sure Pete's gunning for us. Besides, you've done enough. You flew us out of the Macedo compound to the Colombian shore. Then you got us out of Colombia by risking your life walking into the Santa Marta airport. Now it's my turn. This is my problem. Pete is looking for me, not you. You stay with Gaby and I'll sniff around a little and see what I can find. I'll call you often, I promise."

There was a knock at the bedroom door.

"Yes, Rosa, come in," Maggie called out.

224

Rosa walked into the bedroom smiling and carrying a stack of towels.

Rosa paused before entering the bathroom "Hello... Mister Greg...and Maggie...I have...towels."

Learning "I have" had been the key phrase for Rosa this week. Once she had conquered the phrase, she would learn to attach the last word. It was working pretty good until she announced "I have don't" after helping Maggie clean and reorganize her closet. Maggie was still puzzled over what the "don't" meant but decided to forget about it.

The Strongs had brought Rosa home with them after being smuggled into the country. They offered her the right to be on her own, but with no money, no place to live and speaking no English, they knew she would stay with them.

In a couple of months Greg would turn her in as an illegal immigrant, claiming political asylum. The Strong's would sponsor her as their employee. Rosa earned a small salary, room and board and was grateful for the opportunity she was given.

The second Rosa closed the bedroom door behind her, Maggie spoke, hoping to get the upper hand. "So it's settled. You sniff around and I'll watch your back."

Greg shook his head. "No, Maggie, this time it's not your call. I'm insisting you go to Atlanta and hang out with Gaby. It'll only be a day or two at the most. If I come up with nothing, which more than likely will be the case, you can fly to Toccoa and I'll pick you up. I won't take no for an answer."

Realizing that carrying this conversation further would result in an ugly fight, Maggie acquiesced. "I'll call Gaby and then throw a few clothes in a bag. I can be ready in an hour."

***

The trip to Atlanta was uneventful. After a short visit with Gaby, Greg kissed Maggie goodbye and headed home to Cypress.

As he drove north up Interstate 985, he tried to formulate a plan. He surmised the best place to start was with Officer Hudson and then check the bed and breakfast homes in the area. Greg felt Pete wouldn't stay at either of Cypress's two hotels as he knew Greg knew the owners. He needed a picture of Pete and would have to first return home to look through albums from the old days. Then he remembered Pete's face alteration and guessed no one would recognize him from a picture. Since it was already starting to get dark he decided to start his search in the morning.

Greg pulled into his driveway and recalled the night Pete had mysteriously arrived at their home. *Why the hell did he come in the dead of night?* Greg thought as he exited his car. As he approached his house, the realization that he had been gone for over eight hours and Pete could be waiting inside crossed his mind. Then he thought of Rosa and knew she would never let Pete in. She trusted no one and didn't know Pete.

Standing at the front door, Greg shoved his key into the door and hesitated. *What if he overpowered Rosa and was holding her captive?* Greg pondered. He pulled his key from the door and stepped sideways and rang the doorbell. No one came. After a moment, he rang again. *Rosa could be taking a bath,* Greg thought, *after all it was about the time of day that she did that.*

Greg stood leaning against his house adjacent to the front door and pondered his next move. *It'll be dark soon. Maybe I'll wait,* he thought. *Or I could sit in a porch chair and see if Rosa turns on the house lights. But Pete would think of that and turn on the lights himself.*

After a few minutes, Greg made his decision and walked from the porch to his car. He stared back at his home, not knowing for sure he was doing the right thing. Maggie was right. Pete was a scary guy capable of any behavior. Greg seldom ever reacted with such indecisiveness. *When I see him, do I hug him or shoot him?* Greg thought.

Darkness came and someone inside the house turned on the porch light, then the light to their bedroom, then the dining room light. Because the curtains were drawn, Greg couldn't see movement.

He walked from his car back to his front door, rang the bell and waited. No one came. He pulled his service revolver from his waist and inserted the key. He quietly turned the key and pushed the door open. Now he was sure Pete was in the house. Once inside, Greg turned off the living room and porch lights. Lifting his weapon, he crept along the wall, heading for the dining room.

Standing next to the dining room entrance, Greg swung around and entered. It was easy to see the dining room was empty. He could see the only light left on in the house was in his bedroom. This was a moment he wasn't looking forward to.

Pushing the bedroom door open, Greg swung into the

room ready to fire his weapon. Pete wasn't there. Neither was Rosa. He checked the bedroom closets and the adjacent bathroom. *What has he done with Rosa?* Greg wondered as he turned off the light, leaving his house in total darkness.

Greg sat on his bed and rested his weapon in his lap. His mind raced. *Am I going crazy? I don't understand any of this. Where's Pete and where's Rosa? What's next? Maybe I'll turn on every light in this house until I find someone...anyone. I mean, what else is left?*

Greg got up from the bed and groped his way to the light switch next to the bedroom entrance. When he flipped the switch, he was startled to see Pete standing in the doorway pointing a gun at him.

"I've got the drop on you, old friend. Don't try anything stupid. Just lay the gun down real slow," Pete said.

Greg bent over and laid his weapon on the floor next to his feet.

"You know what to do next. Kick the gun toward me," Pete ordered.

Greg complied and, staring into Pete's eyes, asked, "This whole thing was a setup, wasn't it, Pete? While on assignment in Colombia, you became a Macedo lackey and he paid you to set me up...right?"

Pete smiled at his old friend. "You probably don't realize I waited two days until I could catch you alone. I didn't realize you had a live-in housekeeper. Where did you pick her up?"

"It doesn't matter. What have you done with her, Pete?"

"She's in the bathtub...in the other bathroom. She went

crazy when she caught me breaking into the house." Pete said. "I couldn't shut her up. I was as surprised as she was. I had no choice but to kill her. She wouldn't stop screaming. You understand, I'm sure."

"So now what, Pete?" You make Maggie a widow, disappear forever and live out your life in some decrepit third world country on Macedo's money?"

Pete felt he was far enough away from Greg that he could lower his gun to his side before speaking. "The damn Cubans have sent my daughter a death threat. If you're not dead soon, she and her children will be. I guess it would be meaningless for me to apologize and tell you I was stupid to do this. I needed the money and Macedo had plenty of that. Oh, how bad Macedo hated you, almost as much as Harkin." Pete raised his weapon and pointed it at Greg again. "I was told you killed Macedo in the jungle. Congratulations! If Cuba would have let me go without strings, I would have disappeared, like you said, forever. Hey, what the hell, I gave you Harkin."

"How about the Nixon agreement you had with Halderman? Was that a lie also?" Greg asked.

Pete chuckled, moving closer but keeping his weapon pointed at Greg's chest. "What difference does it make, predator man? When I spoke with Raul Castro, he told me he knew the Nixon agreement was for real. I never told him either way. Like I said, what the hell difference does it make?"

Out of the corner of Greg's eye, he saw movement in the darkened dining room. Without warning, Maggie stepped into the doorway, pointing her small snub-nosed revolver at Pete.

"Drop your gun, Pete, cause I'll shoot you as sure as I'm standing here wanting to anyway," Maggie demanded.

Surprised, Pete hesitated before lowering his gun to his side but didn't drop it. He turned to face Maggie.

"Come on, Maggie, you're not going to shoot me. You may be a tough gal, but shooting a friend in cold blood is not something you could do," Pete said, being careful not to move his arm holding his gun. "Why don't you turn around and leave the way you came in and you won't get hurt. This is about Greg and me."

"Don't test me, Pete. I'll shoot your ass. And I'm close enough I won't miss. You know I shoot well. Now drop the damn gun," Maggie ordered.

Pete turned to face Greg. "I didn't come here to kill you, old friend. I came to tell you how sorry I am that I brought you and Maggie into this. I came to tell you that what's left of the money Macedo gave me has now been deposited in your bank account in Cypress. I came to tell you this has gone so far there's no way out for me. I love you, old friend. I'm a fuck up!"

Pete quickly lifted his weapon to his temple and fired. Chunks of Pete's blood, brains and skull spattered Maggie's face. She screamed in horror. Pete fell to the floor dead. Maggie dropped her gun and raced to hug Greg.

"Oh God, Greg, I'm sick. I'm going to throw up," Maggie said, pushing away, leaning forward to vomit.

"Let me take you in the bathroom and clean you up, then I'll call the police. Change your clothes and put them in a bag for the investigators. They'll need it. It's over, Maggie. It's over," Greg announced, giving Maggie a lengthy hug.

Then Greg pushed her away. "Wait a minute. Why in the hell are you here? Can't you do anything I ask?"

Maggie gave her husband a guilty smirk before speaking. "Right after you left Gaby's, I called flight weather and learned I had about four hours before the entire region around Toccoa would be socked in for the next few days. Gaby drove me to the airport and I flew in bad weather to Toccoa. It was a bitch flight. Tom, who runs the Toccoa airport, let me use his car to drive here."

Greg walked with Maggie to the phone in their kitchen. "Hello, Cypress Police, this is Captain Strong at 21 Meadow Wood in Cypress. I want to report a homicide/suicide event at my residence. We're not in danger. Take your time."

CHAPTER NINETEEN

The priest anointed the grave site, Pete's coffin and the small group of mourners standing nearby. "May God grant your servant, Peter Mario Spoto, eternal peace. Oh Lord, forgive him of his sins. May his soul and all the souls of the faithfully departed rest in peace. Amen."

A drop of holy water hit Maggie's lower lip and she immediately reached to wipe it away. She stood expressionless at the coffin. *Is the son-of-a-bitch in there or not?* she thought, squeezing Greg's arm tighter.

Greg looked at her and smiled. He knew what she was thinking. "He's in there, Maggie. I went to the funeral home this morning to check. Relax, it's over," Greg assured her.

As Maggie and Greg got into their car, Pete's daughter approached. "Captain Strong, may I please speak with you?"

Maggie continued to get in their rental car, but Greg

decided to walk a short distance away to have a conversation he was dreading.

"You knew my dad better than anyone, even better than his fellow agents with DEA. What happened to him? He was the best of the best. Why would he kill your housekeeper and himself?" she asked.

Greg ignored the questions and asked, "Are you still getting death threats?"

"No, not for two weeks now. Did my dad tell you about them and what's that all about?" she asked.

"If you get another threat, I want you to call me. I've no answers for you. Your father must've gotten screwed up in his head. I simply don't know. He was a good man and a great DEA agent. Believe me when I say I'll never forget him."

Pete's daughter remained silent and Greg took that opportunity to turn away and walk to his car. The flight home from Miami to Atlanta was quiet and uneventful as was the drive back to Cypress.

That evening, Greg and Maggie went to bed shortly after they got home from the Atlanta airport. Both were exhausted from their round trip flight for the funeral and the hour and a half drive back home. They both drifted off to sleep soon after their heads hit their pillows.

***

Maggie heard it before Greg. She sat up in bed, awakening from a restless sleep. She punched Greg awake. "Listen! Are you hearing what I'm hearing? Is this a nightmare?" Maggie asked.

A car was pulling up in front of their house with its lights on. Maggie looked at the clock and noted it was only ten o'clock. Greg reached for his gun and ran to the dining room window for a better look. Maggie grabbed her small revolver from her nightstand and stood next to him.

A man got out of the car and walked toward the house. Greg dashed to the front door and turned on the porch lights before the man could get to the porch. He waited. After a moment the doorbell rang.

Maggie stayed in the dining room, holding her weapon with both hands at chest level. She could feel her heart pounding.

Holding his gun behind his back, Greg pulled the front door open until the safety chain tightened. He stared at the young man and thought he looked vaguely familiar.

"May I help you? Greg asked.

"Hello, Captain Strong, is that you, sir?" the stranger asked.

"Who's asking, if I may ask?"

Maggie began to move from the dining room to stand next to her husband. She cupped her pistol in the palm of her hand.

"It's Mitch Hammond....from UPS. Is that you, Captain?"

Greg shut the front door and removed the safety chain. He concealed his weapon behind his back and opened the door wide. There stood a man he thought he would never forget but momentarily had done just that.

Greg reached to shake Mitch's hand. When he saw Mitch smile, the handshake turned into a big hug.

"I owe you my life, young man. You're always welcome in my home...come in, please."

He turned to Maggie standing next to him. "You remember Mitch, don't cha, babe?"

Maggie reached out to hug Mitch with her gun still in her right hand. "Of course I do. I'll never forget the man who saved my husband's life. Welcome to our home, Mitch. Come in and let me make you a cup of coffee."

"I'm so sorry to be arriving at such a late hour, but you folks are very hard to find," Mitch said. "Your phone number is unlisted and no one in town would tell me where you live. After telling a policeman the story of how we know each other, he shook his head and said it must be true because no one could make up such a wild tale. He gave me your address and told me how to get here. I hope that was okay. I wouldn't want him to get into trouble."

"How do you take your coffee?" Maggie asked, sliding her pistol into a kitchen drawer and closing it..

"Cream and sugar, please," Mitch responded. "I came to thank you, Captain, for causing my career to skyrocket. After you put me in for citizen of the year, UPS executives took notice of me. They love that kind of publicity and I became the employee who could do no wrong. I even made a UPS commercial and my salary has tripled."

Maggie placed three cups of coffee on the kitchen table and sat next to Greg. "Can you stay a couple of days? We have room," she asked.

"That's very generous of you, Mrs. Strong. I was going to check in at a bed and breakfast but if you have the room, I would be most appreciative of you giving me a place to stay. It'll just be for overnight."

"Good, then it's settled. Let me help you with your luggage," Greg offered.

"Oh, that reminds me. I've a gift for the two of you. It's in the car. Why don't we all go out and Mrs. Strong can carry in my gift while we bring in the luggage?" Mitch suggested.

"Please, don't call me Mrs. Strong. It's Maggie."

The three finished their coffee and walked to Mitch's car.

"I spoke with several officers in Miami Beach and they said you were in poor health. You look great to me. Are you in poor health, Captain?" Mitch asked.

"I was for a while but then I got better. It's a long story I won't bore you with. I hate people who talk about their illnesses all the time so I won't inflict that on you, Mitch."

Mitch reached into the back seat of his car and removed a shoe box with the lid off. He turned and handed it to Maggie.

"Oh my God, Greg! Look at this. How old is he? Or is it a she?" Maggie asked with great excitement.

"It's a she. A full blooded German shepherd and I've her AKC papers in my luggage. I heard from the police department you lost your dog. This is my gift. I hope you don't mind. You're not supposed to give pets as gifts but, in this case, I took the risk,"

Maggie lifted the puppy from the shoebox. "How old is she? She's so tiny."

She was weaned from her mother a week ago," Mitch warned. "She whines a lot at night so I brought a piece of her mother's bedding with her scent on it to put next to her. It seems to help."

While Greg carried the luggage into the house, Maggie cuddled her new puppy to her chest and followed them in. The three returned to the kitchen and Maggie poured a second cup of coffee for everyone, never turning loose of her new puppy.

"I'm pleased you're back in good health, Captain. I was expecting the worse. You look great," Mitch said, taking a sip from his cup.

"Thanks, Mitch, it was slow goin' and I'm never going to be back at one hundred percent but that's okay. Maggie takes good care of me. Thank you so much for buying us the puppy."

"No problem, Captain. How are you handling your retirement? Things must get pretty dull and boring up here in these mountains, especially after all the action you saw as a cop."

Greg looked at Maggie and smiled. "Yeah, Mitch, things do get a bit boring around here."

THE END